PARROT & CO.

Parrot & Co.

By *Harold MacGrath*

Author of

"The Best Man," "The Carpet from Bagdad,"
"The Place of Honeymoons"

With Four Illustrations in Color
By ANDRÉ CASTAIGNE

A. L. BURT COMPANY

PUBLISHERS   NEW YORK

CONTENTS

PARROT & CO.

PARROT & CO.

I

IT began somewhere in the middle of the world, between London which is the beginning and New York which is the end, where all things are east of the one and west of the other. To be precise, a forlorn landing on the west bank of the muddy. turbulent Irrawaddy, remembered by man only so often as it was necessary for the flotilla boat to call for paddy, a visiting commissioner anxious to get away, or a family homeward-bound. Somewhere in the northeast was Mandalay, but lately known in romance, verse and song; somewhere in the southeast lay Prome, known only in guide-books and time-tables; and farther south, Rangoon, sister to Singapore, the half-way house of the derelicts of the world. On the east side of the river, over there, was a semblance of civilization. That is to say, men wore white linen, avoided murder, and frequently paid their gambling debts. But on this west side stood wilderness, not the kind one reads about as being eventually conquered by white men; no, the real grim desolation, where the ax cuts but leaves no blaze, where the pioneer disappears and few or none follow. The pioneer has always been a successful pugilist, but in this part of Burma fate, out of pure admiration for the pygmy's gameness, decided to call the battle a draw. It was not the wilderness of the desert, of the jungle; rather the tragic hopeless state of a settlement that neither progressed, retarded, nor stood still.

Between the landing and the settlement itself there stretched a winding road, arid and treeless, perhaps two miles in length. It announced definitely that its end was futility. All this day long heavy bullock-carts had rumbled over it, rumbled toward the landing and rattled emptily back to the settlement. The dust hung like a fog above the road, not only for this day, but for all days between the big rains. Each night, however, the cold heavy dews drew it down, cooling but never congealing it. From under the first footfall the next day it rose again. When the gods, or the elements, or Providence, arranged the world as a fit habitation for man, India and Burma were made the dust-bins. And as water finds its levels, so will dust, earthly and human, the quick and the dead.

It was after five in the afternoon. The sun was sinking, hazily but swiftly; ribbons of scarlet, ribbons of rose, ribbons of violet, lay one upon the other. The sun possessed no definite circle; a great blinding radiance like metal pouring from the mouth of a blast-furnace. Along the road walked two men, phantom-like. One saw their heads dimly and still more dimly their bodies to the knees; of legs, there was nothing visible. Occasionally they stepped aside to permit some bullock-cart to pass. One of them swore, not with any evidence of temper, not viciously, but in a kind of mechanical protest, which, from long usage, had become a habit. He directed these epithets never at animate things, never at anything he could by mental or physical contest overcome. He swore at the dust, at the heat, at the wind, at the sun.

The other wayfarer, with the inherent patience

3

of his blood, said nothing and waited, setting down the heavy kit-bag and the canvas-valise (his own). When the way was free again he would sling the kit-bag and the valise over his shoulder and step back into the road. His turban, once white, was brown with dust and sweat. His khaki uniform was rent under the arm-pits, several buttons were gone; his stockings were rusty black, mottled with patches of brown skin; and the ragged canvas-shoes spurted little spirals of dust as he walked. The British-Indian government had indulgently permitted him to proceed about his duties as guide and carrier under the cognomen of James Hooghly, in honor of a father whose surname need not be written here, and in further honor of the river upon which, quite inconveniently one early morning, he had been born. For he was Eurasian; half European, half Indian, having his place twixt heaven and hell, which is to say, nowhere. His father had died of a complication of bhang-drinking and opium-eating; and as a consequence, James was full of humorless imagination, spells of moodiness and outbursts of hilarious politics. Every native who acquires a facility in English immediately sets out to rescue

India from the clutches of the British raj, occasionally advancing so far as to send a bullet into some harmless individual in the Civil Service.

James was faithful, willing and strong; and as a carrier of burdens, took unmurmuringly his place beside the tireless bullock and the elephant. He was a Methodist; why, no one could find lucid answer, since he ate no beef, drank from no common cup, smoked through his fist when he enjoyed a pipe, and never assisted Warrington Sahib in his deadly pursuit of flies and mosquitoes. He was Hindu in all his acts save in his manner of entering temples; in this, the European blood kept his knees unbended. By dint of inquiry his master had learned that James looked upon his baptism and conversion in Methodism as a corporal would have looked upon the acquisition of a V. C. Twice, during fever and plague, he had saved his master's life. With the guilelessness of the Oriental he considered himself responsible for his master in all future times. Instead of paying off a debt he had acquired one. Treated as he was, kindly but always firmly, he would have surrendered his life cheerfully at the beck of the white man.

PARROT & CO.

Warrington was an American. He was also one of those men who never held misfortune in contempt, whose outlook wherever it roamed was tolerant. He had patience for the weak, resolution for the strong, and a fearless amiability toward all. He was like the St. Bernard dog, very difficult to arouse. It is rather the way with all men who are strong mentally and physically. He was tall and broad and deep. Under the battered pith-helmet his face was as dark as the Eurasian's; but the eyes were blue, bright and small-pupiled, as they are with men who live out-of-doors, who are compelled of necessity to note things moving in the distances. The nose was large and well-defined. All framed in a tangle of blond beard and mustache which, if anything, added to the general manliness of his appearance. He, too, wore khaki, but with the addition of tan riding-leggings, which had seen anything but rocking-horse service. The man was yellow from the top of his helmet to the soles of his shoes — outside. For the rest, he was a mystery, to James, to all who thought they knew him, and most of all to himself. A pariah, an outcast, a fugitive from the bloodless hand of the law; a gentleman

6

born, once upon a time a clubman, college-bred; a
contradiction, a puzzle for which there was not any
solution, not even in the hidden corners of the
man's heart. His name wasn't Warrington; and
he had rubbed elbows with the dregs of humanity,'
and still looked you straight in the eye because he
had come through inferno without bringing any of
the defiling pitch.

From time to time he paused to relight his crumbling cheroot. The tobacco was strong and bitter,
and stung his parched lips; but the craving for the
tang of the smoke on his tongue was not to be
denied.

Under his arm he carried a small iron-cage, pat-
terned something like a rat-trap. It contained a
Rajputana parrakeet, not much larger than a robin,
but possessor of a soul as fierce as that of Palladin,
minus, however, the smoothing influence of chivalry. He had been born under the eaves of the
scarlet palace in Jaipur (so his history ran); but
the proximity of Indian princes had left him un-
touched: he had neither chivalry, politeness, nor
diplomacy. He was, in fact, thoroughly and con-
sistently bad. Round and round he went, over and

7

over, top-side, down-side, restlessly. For at this moment he was hearing those familiar evening sounds which no human ear can discern: the mutterings of the day-birds about to seek cover for the night. In the field at the right of the road stood a lonely tree. It was covered with brilliant scarlet leaves and blossoms, and justly the natives call it the Flame of the Jungle. A flock of small birds were gyrating above it.

"Jah, jah, jah! Jah—jah—ja-a-a-h!" cried the parrot, imitating the Burmese bell-gong that calls to prayer. Instantly he followed the call with a shriek so piercing as to sting the ear of the man who was carrying him.

"You little son-of-a-gun," he laughed; "where do you pack away all that noise?"

There was a strange bond between the big yellow man and this little green bird. The bird did not suspect it, but the man knew. The pluck, the pugnacity and the individuality of the feathered comrade had been an object lesson to the man, at a time when he had been on the point of throwing up the fight.

"Jah, jah, jah! Jah—jah—ja-a-a-h!" The

8

bird began its interminable somersaults, pausing only to reach for the tantalizing finger of the man, who laughed again as he withdrew the digit in time.

For six years he had carried the bird with him, through India and Burma and Malacca, and not yet had he won a sign of surrender. There were many scars on his forefingers. It was amazing. With one pressure of his hand he could have crushed out the life of the bird, but over its brave unconquerable spirit he had no power. And that is why he loved it.

Far away in the past they had met. He remembered the day distinctly and bitterly. He had been on the brink of self-destruction. Fever and poverty and terrible loneliness had battered and beaten him flat into the dust from which this time he had had no wish to rise. He had walked out to the railway station at Jaipur to witness the arrival of the tourist train from Ahmadabad. He wanted to see white men and white women from his own country, though up to this day he had carefully avoided them. (How he hated the English, with their cold-blooded suspicion of all who were not island-born!) The natives surged about the train, with brass-ware, antique articles of warfare, tiger-hunting knives (accompanied by perennial fairy tales), skins and silks. There were beggars, holy men, guides and fakirs.

Squatted in the dust before the door of a first-class carriage was a solemn brown man, in turban and clout, exhibiting performing parrots. It was Rajah's turn. He fired a cannon, turned somersaults through a little steel-hoop, opened a tiny chest, took out a four-anna piece, carried it to his master, and in exchange received some seed. Thereupon he waddled resentfully back to the iron-cage, opened the door, closed it behind him, and began to mutter belligerently. Warrington haggled for two straight hours. When he returned to his sordid evil-smelling lodgings that night, he possessed the parrot and four rupees, and sat up the greater part of the night trying to make the bird perform his tricks. The idea of suicide no longer bothered him; trifling though it was, he had found an interest in life. And on the morrow came the Eurasian, who trustfully loaned Warrington every coin that he could scrape together.

Often, in the dreary heart-achy days that followed, when weeks passed ere he saw the face of a white man, when he had to combat opium and bhang and laziness in the natives under him, the bird and his funny tricks had saved him from whisky, or worse. In camp he gave Rajah much freedom, its wings being clipt; and nothing pleased the little rebel so much as to claw his way up to his master's shoulder, sit there and watch the progress of the razor, with intermittent " jawing " at his own reflection in the cracked hand-mirror.

Up and down the Irrawaddy, at the rest-houses, on the boats, to those of a jocular turn of mind the three were known as " Parrot & Co." Warrington's amiability often misled the various scoundrels with whom he was at times forced to associate. A man who smiled most of the time and talked Hindustani to a parrot was not to be accorded much courtesy; until one day Warrington had settled all distinctions, finally and primordially, with the square of his fists. After that he went his way unmolested, having soundly trounced one of the biggest bullies in the teak timber-yards at Rangoon.

He made no friends; he had no confidences to exchange; nor did he offer to become the repository of other men's pasts. But he would share his bread and his rupees, when he had them, with any who asked. Many tried to dig into his past, but he was as unresponsive as granite. It takes a woman to find out what a man is and has been; and Warrington went about women in a wide circle. In a way he was the most baffling kind of a mystery to those who knew him: he frequented the haunts of men, took a friendly drink, played cards for small sums, laughed and jested like any other anchorless man. In the East men are given curious names. They become known by phrases, such as, The Man Who Talks, Mr. Once Upon a Time, The One-Rupee Man, and the like. As Warrington never received any mail, as he never entered a hotel, nor spoke of the past, he became The Man Who Never Talked of Home.

"I say, James, old sport, no more going up and down this bally old river. We'll go on to Rangoon to-night, if we can find a berth."

"Yes, Sahib; this business very piffle," replied the Eurasian without turning his head. Two things he dearly loved to acquire: a bit of American slang and a bit of English silver. He was invariably changing his rupees into shillings, and Warrington could not convince him that he was always losing in the transactions.

They tramped on through the dust. The sun dropped. A sudden chill began to penetrate the haze. The white man puffed his cheroot, its wrapper dangling; the servant hummed an Urdu lullaby; the parrot complained unceasingly.

" How much money have you got, James? "

" Three annas."

Warrington laughed and shook the dust from his beard. " It's a great world, James, a great and wonderful world. I've just two rupees myself. In other words, we are busted."

" Two rupees! " James paused and turned. " Why, Sahib, you have three hundred thousand rupees in your pocket."

" But not worth an anna until I get to Rangoon. Didn't those duffers give you anything for handling their luggage the other day? "

" Not a pice, Sahib."

" Rotters! It takes an Englishman to turn a small trick like that. Well, well; there were extenuating circumstances. They had sore heads. No man likes to pay three hundred thousand for something he could have bought for ten thousand. And I made them come to me, James, to me. I made them come to this god-forsaken hole, just because it pleased my fancy. When you have the skewer in, always be sure to turn it around. I believe I'm heaven-born after all. The Lord hates a quitter, and so do I. I nearly quit myself, once; eh, Rajah, old top? But I made them come to me. That's the milk in the cocoanut, the curry on the rice. They almost had me. Two rupees! It truly is a great world."

"Jah, jah, jah! Jah—jah—jah—ja-a-a-h!" screamed the parrot. "*Chaloo!*"

"Go on! That's the ticket. If I were a praying man, this would be the time for it. Three hundred thousand rupees!" The man looked at the far horizon, as if he would force his gaze beyond, into the delectable land, the Eden out of which he had been driven. "Caviar and truffles, and Romanée Conti, and Partagas!"

"Chicken and curry and Scotch whisky."

"Bah! You've the imagination of a he-goat."

"All right, Sahib."

"James, I owe you three hundred rupees, and I

am going to add seven hundred more. We've been fighting this old top for six years together, and you've been a good servant and a good friend; and I'll take you with me as far as this fortune will go, if you say the word."

"Ah, Sahib, I am much sorry. But Delhi calls, and I go. A thousand rupees will make much business for me in the Chandney Chowk."

"Just as you say."

Presently they became purple shades in a brown world.

II

A MAN WITH A PAST

THE moonless Oriental night, spangled with large and brilliant stars, brilliant yet mellow, unlike the crisp scintillating presentment in northern latitudes, might have served as an illustration of an air-tight bowl, flung down relentlessly upon this part of the world. Inside this figurative bowl it ,was chill, yet the air was stirless. It was without refreshment; it became a labor and not an exhilaration to breath it. A pall of suffocating dust rolled above and about the Irrawaddy flotilla boat which, buffeted by the strong irregular current, strained at its cables, now at the bow, now at the stern, not dissimilar to the last rocking of a deserted swing. This sensation was quite perceptible to the girl who leaned over the bow-rail, her handkerchief pressed to her nose, and gazed interestedly at the steep bank, up and down which the sweating coolies swarmed like Gargantuan rats. They clawed and scrambled up and slid and shuffled down; and always the bank threatened to slip and carry them all into the swirling murk below. A dozen torches were stuck into the ground above the crumbling ledge; she saw the flames as one sees a burning match cupped in a smoker's hands, shedding light upon nothing save that which stands immediately behind it.

She choked a little. Her eyes smarted. Her lips were slightly cracked, and cold-cream seemed only to provide a surer resting place for the impalpable dust. It had penetrated her clothes; it had percolated through wool and linen and silk, intimately, until three baths a day had become a welcome routine, providing it was possible to obtain water. Water. Her tongue ran across her lips. Oh, for a drink from the old cold pure spring at home! Tea, coffee, and bottled soda; nothing that ever touched the thirsty spots in her throat.

She looked up at the stars and they looked down upon her, but what she asked they could not, would not, answer. Night after night she had asked, and night after night they had only twinkled as of old. She had traveled now for four months, and still the doubt beset her. It was to be a leap in the dark, with no one to tell her what was on the other side. But why this insistent doubt? Why could she not take the leap gladly, as a woman should who had given the affirmative to a man? With him she was certain that she loved him, away from him she did not know what sentiment really abided in her heart. She was wise enough to realize that something was wrong; and there were but three months between her and the inevitable decision. Never before had she known other than momentary indecision; and it irked her to find that her clarity of vision was fallible and human like the rest of her. The truth was, she didn't know her mind. She shrugged, and the movement stirred the dust that had gathered upon her shoulders.

What a dust-ridden, poverty-ridden, plague-ridden world she had seen! Ignorance wedded to superstition, yet waited upon by mystery and romance and incomparable beauty. As the Occidental thought rarely finds analysis in the Oriental mind, so her mind could not gather and understand this amalgamation of art and ignorance. She forgot that another race of men had built those palaces and temples and forts and tombs, and that they

had vanished as the Greeks and Romans have vanished, leaving only empty spaces behind, which the
surviving tribes neither fill nor comprehend.

"A rare old lot of dust; eh, Miss Chetwood? I
wish we could travel by night, but you can't trust
this blooming old Irrawaddy after sundown.
Charts are so much waste-paper. You just have
to _know_ the old lady. Bars rise in a night, shift
this side and that. But the days are all right. No
dust when you get in mid-stream. What?"

"I never cease wondering how those poor coolies
can carry those heavy rice-bags," she replied to the
purser.

"Oh, they are used to it," carelessly.

The great gray stack of paddy-bags seemed, in
the eyes of the girl, fairly to melt away.

"By Jove!" exclaimed the purser. "There's
Parrot & Co.!" He laughed and pointed toward
one of the torches.

"Parrot & Co.? I do not understand."

"That big blond chap behind the fourth torch.
Yes, there. Sometime I'll tell you about him. Picturesque duffer."

PARROT & CO.

She could have shrieked aloud, but all she did was to draw in her breath with a gasp that went so deep it gave her heart a twinge. Her fingers tightened upon the teak-rail. Suddenly she knew, and was ashamed of her weakness. It was simply a remarkable likeness, nothing more than that; it could not possibly be anything more. Still, a ghost could not have startled her as this living man had done.

"Who is he?"

"A chap named Warrington. But over here that signifies nothing; might just as well be Jones or Smith or Brown. We call him Parrot & Co., but the riff-raff have another name for him. The Man Who Never Talked of Home. For two or three seasons he's been going up and down the river. Ragged at times, prosperous at others. Lately it's been rags. He's always carrying that Rajputana parrot. You've seen the kind around the palaces and forts: saber-blade wings, long tail-feathers, green and blue and scarlet, and the ugliest little rascals going. This one is trained to do tricks."

"But the man!" impatiently.

He eyed her, mildly surprised. "Oh, he puzzles us all a bit, you know. Well educated; somewhere back a gentleman; from the States. Of course I don't know; something shady, probably. They don't tramp about like this otherwise. For all that, he's rather a decent sort; no bounder like that rotter we left at Mandalay. He never talks about himself. I fancy he's lonesome again."

" Lonesome? "

" It's the way, you know. These poor beggars drop aboard for the night, merely to see a white woman again, to hear decent English, to dress and dine like a human being. They disappear the next day, and often we never see them again."

" What do they do? " The question came to her lips mechanically.

" Paddy-fields. White men are needed to oversee them. And then, there's the railway, and there's the new oil-country north of Prome. You'll see the wells to-morrow. Rather fancy this Warrington chap has been working along the new pipe-lines. They're running them down to Rangoon. Well, there goes the last bag. Will you excuse me? The lading bills, you know. If he's with us to-morrow, I'll have him put the parrot through its turns. An amusing little beggar."

" Why not introduce him to me? "

" Beg pardon? "

" I'm not afraid," quietly.

" By Jove, no! But this is rather difficult, you know. If he shouldn't turn out right. . . ." with commendable hesitance.

" I'll take all the responsibility. It's a whim."

" Well, you American girls are the eighth wonder of the world." The purser was distinctly annoyed. " And it may be an impertinence on my part, but I never yet saw an American woman who would accept advice or act upon it."

" Thanks. What would you advise? " with dangerous sweetness.

" Not to meet this man. It's irregular. I know nothing about him. If you had a father or a brother on board. . . ."

" Or even a husband! " laughing.

" There you are! " resignedly. " You laugh. You women go everywhere, and half the time unprotected."

" Never quite unprotected. We never venture beyond the call of gentlemen."

"That is true," brightening. "You insist on meeting this chap?"

"I do not insist; only, I am bored, and he might interest me for an hour." She added: "Besides, it may annoy the others."

The purser grinned reluctantly. "You and the colonel don't get on. Well, I'll introduce this chap at dinner. If I don't. . . ."

"I am fully capable of speaking to him without any introduction whatever." She laughed again. "It will be very kind of you."

When he had gone she mused over this impulse so alien to her character. An absolute stranger, a man with a past, perhaps a fugitive from justice; and because he looked like Arthur Ellison, she was seeking his acquaintance. Something, then, could break through her reserve and aloofness? She had traveled from San Francisco to Colombo, unattended save by an elderly maiden who had risen by gradual stages from nurse to companion, but who could not be made to remember that she was no longer a nurse. In all these four months Elsa had not made half a dozen acquaintances, and of these

23

'she had not sought one. Yet, she was asking to meet a stranger whose only recommendation was a singular likeness to another man. The purser was right. It was very irregular.

"Parrot & Co.!" she murmured. She searched among the phantoms moving to and fro upon the ledge; but the man with the cage was gone. It was really uncanny.

She dropped her arms from the rail and went to her stateroom and dressed for dinner. She did not give her toilet any particular care. There was no thought of conquest, no thought of dazzling the man in khaki. It was the indolence and carelessness of the East, where clothes become only necessities and are no longer the essentials of adornment.

Elsa Chetwood was twenty-five, lithely built, outwardly reposeful, but dynamic within. Education, environment and breeding had somewhat smothered the glowing fires. She was a type of the ancient repression of woman, which finds its exceptions in the Aspasias and Helens and Cleopatras of legend and history. In features she looked exactly what she was, well-bred and well-born. Beauty she also had, but it was the cold beauty of northern winter nights.

A MAN WITH A PAST

It compelled admiration rather than invited it. Spiritually, Elsa was asleep. The fire was there, the gift of loving greatly, only it smoldered, without radiating even the knowledge of its presence. Men loved her, but in awe, as one loves the marbles of Phidias. She knew no restraint, and yet she had passed through her stirless years restrained. She was worldly without being more than normally cynical; she was rich without being either frugal or extravagant. Her independence was inherent and not acquired. She had laid down certain laws for herself to follow; and that these often clashed with the laws of convention, which are fetish to those who divide society into three classes, only mildly amused her. Right from wrong she knew, and that sufficed her.

Her immediate relatives were dead; those who were distantly related remained so, as they had no part in her life nor she in theirs. Relatives, even the best of them, are practically strangers to us. They have their own affairs and interests, and if these touch ours it is generally through the desire to inherit what we have. So Elsa went her way alone. From her father she had inherited a remarkable and seldom errant judgment. To her, faces were generally book-covers, they repelled or attracted; and she found large and undiminishing interest in the faculty of pressing back the covers and reading the text. Often battered covers held treasures, and often the editions de luxe were swindles. But in between the battered covers and the exquisite Florentine hand-tooling there ranged a row of mediocre books; and it was among these that Elsa found that her instinct was not wholly infallible, as will be seen.

To-day she was facing the first problem of her young life, epochal. She was, as it were, to stop and begin life anew. And she didn't know, she wasn't sure.

There were few passengers aboard. There were three fussy old English maidens under the protection of a still fussier old colonel, who disagreed with everybody because his liver disagreed with him. Twenty years of active service in Upper India had seriously damaged that physiological function, and "pegs" no longer mellowed him. The quartet greatly amused Elsa. Their nods were abrupt, and they spoke in the most formal manner. She was un-

der grave suspicion; in the first place, she was traveling alone, in the second place, she was an American.
At table there was generally a desultory conversation, and many a barb of malice Elsa shot from her
bow. Figuratively, the colonel walked about like
a porcupine, bristling with arrows instead of quills.
Elsa could have shouted at times, for the old war-
dog was perfectly oblivious. There was, besides,
the inevitable German tourist, who shelled with
questions every man who wore brass-buttons, until
there was some serious talk of dropping him astern
some day. He had shelled the colonel, but that
gentleman was snugly encased in the finest and most
impenetrable Bessemer, complacency.

Upon these Irrawaddy boats the purser is usually
the master of ceremonies in the dining-saloon. The
captain and his officers rarely condescended. Perhaps it was too much trouble to dress; perhaps tourists had disgusted them with life; at any rate, they
remained in obscurity.

Elsa usually sat at the purser's right, and to-night
she found the stranger sitting quietly at her side.
The chair had been vacant since the departure from
Mandalay. Evidently the purser had decided to be

thorough in regard to her wishes. It would look less conspicuous to make the introduction in this manner. And she wanted to meet this man who had almost made her cry out in astonishment.

" Miss Chetwood, Mr. Warrington." This was as far as the purser would unbend.

The colonel's eyes popped; the hands of the three maidens fluttered. Warrington bowed awkwardly, for he was decidedly confused.

" Ha! " boomed the German. " Vat do you tink uff . . . ."

And from soup to coffee Warrington eluded, dodged, stepped under and ran around the fusillade of questions.

Elsa laughed softly. There were breathing-spells, to be sure. Under the cover of this verbal bombardment she found time to inspect the stranger. The likeness, so close at hand, started a ringing in her ears and a flutter in her throat. It was almost unbelievable. He was bigger, broader, his eyes were keener, but there was only one real difference: this man was rugged, whereas Arthur was elegant. It was as if nature had taken two forms from the same mold, and had finished but one of them. His voice was not unpleasant, but there were little sharp points of harshness in it, due quite possibly to the dust.

"I am much interested in that little parrot of yours. I have heard about him."

" Oh! I suppose you've heard what they call us?" His eyes looked straight into hers, smilingly.

" Parrot & Co.? Yes. Will you show him off to-morrow?"

" I shall be very happy to."

But all the while he was puzzling over the purser's unaccountable action in deliberately introducing him to this brown-eyed, golden-skinned young woman. Never before had such a thing occurred upon these boats. True, he had occasionally been spoken to; an idle question flung at him, like a bare bone to a dog. If flung by an Englishman, he answered it courteously, and subsided. He had been snubbed too many times not to have learned this lesson. It never entered his head that the introduction might have been brought about by the girl's interest. He was too mortally shy of women to conceive of such a possibility. So his gratitude was extended to the purser, who, on his side, regretted his good-natured recommendations of the previous hour.

When Elsa learned that the man at her side was to proceed to Rangoon, she ceased to ask him any more questions. She preferred to read her books slowly. Once, while he was engaging the purser, her glance ran over his clothes. She instantly berated her impulsive criticism as a bit of downright caddishness. The lapels of the coat were shiny, the sleeves were short, there was a pucker across the shoulders; the winged-collar gave evidence of having gone to the native laundry once too often; the studs in the shirt-bosom were of the cheapest mother-of-pearl, and the cuff-buttons, ordinary rupee silver. The ensemble suggested that since the purchase of these habiliments of civilization the man had grown, expanded.

Immediately after dinner she retired to her stateroom, conscious that her balance needed readjusting. She had heard and read much lore concerning reincarnation, skeptically; yet here, within call of her voice, was Arthur, not the shadow of a substance, but Arthur, shorn of his elegance, his soft lazy voice, his half-dreaming eyes, his charming indolence. Why should this man's path cross hers, out of all the millions that ran parallel?

She opened her window and looked up at the stars again. She saw one fall, describe an arc and vanish. She wondered what this man had done to put him beyond the pale; for few white men remained in Asia from choice. She had her ideas of what a rascal should be; but Warrington agreed in no essential. It was not possible that dishonor lurked behind those frank blue eyes. She turned from the window, impatiently, and stared at one of her kitbags. Suddenly she knelt down and threw it open, delved among the soft fabrics and silks and produced a photograph. She had not glanced at it during all these weeks. There had been a purpose back of this apparent neglect. The very thing she dreaded happened. Her pulse beat on, evenly, unstirred. She was a failure.

In the photograph the man's beard was trimmed Valois; the beard of the man who had sat next to her at dinner had grown freely and naturally, full. Such a beard was out of fashion, save among country doctors. It signified carelessness, indifference, or a full life wherein the niceties of the razor had of necessity been ignored. Keenly she searched the familiar likeness. What an amazing freak of nature! It was unreal. She tossed the photograph back into the kit-bag, bewildered, uneasy.

Meantime Warrington followed the purser into his office. "I haven't paid for my stateroom yet," he said.

"I'll make it out at once. Rangoon, I understand?"

"Yes. But I'm in a difficulty. I have nothing in change but two rupees."

The purser froze visibly. The tale was trite in his ears.

"But I fancy I've rather good security to offer," went on Warrington coolly. He drew from his wallet a folded slip of paper and spread it out.

The purser stared at it, enchanted. Warrington stared down at the purser, equally enchanted.

"By Jove!" the former gasped finally. "And so you're the chap who's been holding up the oil syndicate all these months? And you're the chap who made them come to this bally landing three days ago?"

"I'm the chap."

A MAN WITH A PAST

It was altogether a new purser who looked up. "Twenty thousand pounds about, and only two rupees in your pocket! Well, well; it takes the East to bowl a man over like this. A certified check on the Bank of Burma needs no further recommendation. In the words of your countrymen, go as far as you like. You can pay me in Rangoon. Your boy takes deck-passage?"

"Yes," returning the check to the wallet.

"Smoke?"

"Shouldn't mind. Thanks."

"Now, sit down and spin the yarn. It must be jolly interesting."

"I'll admit that it has been a tough struggle; but I knew that I had the oil. Been flat broke for months. Had to borrow my boy's savings for food and shelter. Well, this is the way it runs." Warrington told it simply, as if it were a great joke.

"Rippin'! By Jove, you Americans are hard customers to put over. I suppose you'll be setting out for the States at once?" with a curious glance.

"I haven't made any plans yet," eying the cheroot thoughtfully.

"I see." The purser nodded. It was not dif-

33

ficult to understand. "Well, good luck to you wherever you go."

"Much obliged."

Alone in his stateroom Warrington took out Rajah and tossed him on the counterpane of the bed.

"Now, then, old sport!" tapping the parrot on the back with the perch which he used as a baton. Blinking and muttering, the bird performed his tricks, and was duly rewarded and returned to his home of iron. "She'll be wanting to take you home with her, but you're not for sale."

He then opened his window and leaned against the sill, looking up at the stars. But, unlike the girl, he did not ask any questions.

"Free!" he said softly.

III

T HE day began white and chill, for February
nights and mornings are not particularly
comfortable on the Irrawaddy. The boat sped
down the river, smoothly and noiselessly. For all
that the sun shone, the shore-lines were still black.
The dust had not yet risen. Elsa passed through
the dining-saloon to the stern-deck and paused at the
door. The scene was always a source of interest
to her. There were a hundred or more natives
squatting in groups on the deck. They were
wrapped in ragged shawls, cotton rugs of many col-
ors, and woolen blankets, and their turbans were as
bright and colorful as a Holland tulip-bed. Some
of them were smoking long pipes and using their
fists as mouthpieces; others were scrubbing their
teeth with short sticks of fibrous wood; and still
others were eating rice and curry out of little copper pots. There were very few Burmese among

them. They were Hindus, from Central and Southern India, with a scattering of Cingalese. Whenever a Hindu gets together a few rupees, he travels.
He neither cares exactly where the journey ends,
nor that he may never be able to return; so long as
there is a temple at his destination, that suffices him.
The past is the past, to-morrow is to-morrow, but
to-day is to-day: he lives and works and travels,
prisoner to this creed.

Elsa never strolled among them. She was
dainty. This world and these people were new and
strange to her, and as yet she could not quite domi-
nate the fear that some one of these brown-skinned
beings might be coming down with the plague. So
she stood framed in the doorway, a picture rare indeed to the dark eyes that sped their frank glances
in her direction.

"No, Sahib, no; it is three hundred."

"James, I tell you it's rupees three hundred and
twelve, annas eight."

Upon a bench, backed against the partition, almost within touch of her hand, sat the man Warrington and his servant, arguing over their accounts.
The former's battered helmet was tilted at a com-

fortable angle and an ancient cutty hung pendent from his teeth, an idle wisp of smoke hovering over the blackened bowl.

Elsa quietly returned to her chair in the bow and tried to become interested in a novel. By and by the book slipped from her fingers to her lap, and her eyes closed. But not for long. She heard the rasp of a camp-stool being drawn toward her.

"You weren't dozing, were you?" asked the purser apologetically.

"Not in the least. I have only just got up."

"Shouldn't have disturbed you; but your orders were that whenever I had an interesting story about the life over here, I was to tell it to you instantly. And this one is just rippin'!"

"Begin," said Elsa. She sat up and threw back her cloak, for it was now growing warm. "It's about Parrot & Co., I'm sure."

"You've hit it off the first thing," admiringly.

"Well, go on."

"It's better than any story you'll read in a month of Sundays. Our man has just turned the trick, as you Americans say, for twenty thousand pounds."

"Why, that is a fortune!"

"For some of us, yes. You see, whatever he was in the past, it was something worth while, I fancy. Engineering, possibly. Knew his geology and all that. Been wondering for months what kept him hanging around this bally old river. Seems he found oil, borrowed the savings of his servant and bought up some land on the line of the new discoveries. Then he waited for the syndicate to buy. They ignored him. They didn't send any one even to investigate his claim. Stupid, rather. After a while, he went to them, at Prome, at Rangoon. They thought they knew his kind. Ten thousand rupees was all he asked. They laughed. The next time he wanted a hundred thousand. They laughed again. Then he left for the teak forests. He had to live. He came back in four months. In the meantime they had secretly investigated. They offered him fifty thousand. *He* laughed. He wanted two hundred thousand. They advised him to raise cocoanuts. What do you suppose he did then?"

"Got some other persons interested."

"Right-o! Some Americans in Rangoon said

they'd take it over for two hundred thousand. Something about the deal got into the newspapers. The American oil men sent over a representative. That settled the syndicate. What they could have originally purchased for ten thousand they paid three hundred thousand."

"Splendid!" cried Elsa, clapping her hands. She could see it all, the quiet determination of the man, the penury of the lean years, his belief in himself and in what he had found, and the disinterested loyalty of the servant. "Sometimes I wish I were a man and could do things like that."

"Recollect that landing last night?"

Elsa's gesture signified that she was glad to be miles to the south of it.

"Well, he wasn't above having his revenge. He made the syndicate come up there. They wired asking why he couldn't come on to Rangoon. And very frankly he gave his reasons. They came up on one boat and left on another. They weren't very pleasant, but they bought his oil-lands. He came aboard last night with a check for twenty thousand pounds and two rupees in his pocket.

The two rupees were all he had in this world at the time they wrote him the check. Arabian night; what?"

"I am glad. I like pluck; I like endurance; I like to see the lone man win against odds. Tell me, is he going back to America?"

"Ah, there's the weak part in the chain." The purser looked diffidently at the deck floor. It would have been easy enough to discuss the Warrington of yesterday, to offer an opinion as to his past; but the Warrington of this morning was backed by twenty thousand good English sovereigns; he was a different individual, a step beyond the casual damnation of the mediocre. "He says he doesn't know what his plans will be. Who knows? Perhaps some one ran away with his best girl. I've known lots of them to wind up out here on that account."

"Is it a rule, then, that disappointed lovers fly hither, penniless?"

The mockery escaped the purser, who was a good fellow in his blundering way. "Chaps gamble, you know. And this part of the world is full of fleas and mosquitoes and gamblers. When a man's been chucked, he's always asking what's trumps. He's not keen on the game; and the professional gambler takes advantage of his condition. Oh, there are a thousand ways out here of getting rid of your money when the girl's given you the go-by!"

"To that I agree. When do we reach Prome?"

"About six," understanding that the Warrington incident was closed. "It isn't worth while going ashore, though. Nothing to see at night."

"I have no inclination to leave the boat until we reach Rangoon."

She met Warrington at luncheon, and she greeted him amiably. To her mind there was something pitiful in the way the man had tried to improve his condition. Buttons had been renewed, some with black thread and some with white; and there were little islands of brown yarn, at the elbows, at the bottom of the pockets, along the seams. So long as she lived, no matter whom she might marry, she was convinced that never would the thought of this man fade completely from her memory. Neither the amazing likeness nor the romantic background had anything to do with this conviction. It was the man's utter loneliness.

"I have been waiting for Parrot & Co. all the morning," she said.

"I'll show him to you right after luncheon. It wasn't that I had forgotten."

She nodded; but he did not comprehend that this inclination of the head explained that she knew the reason of the absence. She could in fancy see the strong brown fingers clumsily striving to thread the needle. (As a matter of fact, her imagination was at fault. James had done the greater part of the repairing.)

Rajah took the center of the stage; and even the colonel forgot his liver long enough to chuckle when the bird turned somersaults through the steel-hoop. Elsa was delighted. She knelt and offered him her slim white finger. Rajah eyed it with his head cocked at one side. He turned insolently and entered his cage. Since he never saw a finger without flying at it in a rage, it was the politest thing he had ever done.

"Isn't he a sassy little beggar?" laughed the

owner. " That's the way; his hand, or claw, rather, against all the world. I've had him half a dozen years, and he hates me just as thoroughly now as he did when I picked him up while I was at Jaipur."

" Have you carried him about all this time?" demanded the colonel.

" He was one of the two friends I had, one of the two I trusted," quietly, with a look which rather disconcerted the Anglo-Indian.

" By the actions of him I should say that he was your bitterest enemy."

" He is; yet I call him friend. There's a peculiar thing about friendship," said the kneeling man. " We make a man our friend; we take him on trust, frankly and loyally; we give him the best we have in us; but we never really know. Rajah is frankly my enemy, and that's why I love him and trust him. I should have preferred a dog; but one takes what one can. Besides . . ." Warrington paused, thrust the perch between the bars, and got up.

" Jah, jah, jah! Jah—jah—ja-a-a-h!" the bird shrilled.

"Oh, what a funny little bird!" cried Elsa, laughing. "What does he say?"

"I've often wondered. It sounds like the bell-gong you hear in the Shwe Dagon Pagoda, in Rangoon. He picked it up himself."

The colonel returned to his elderly charges and became absorbed in his aged *Times*. If the girl wanted to pick up the riff-raff to talk to, that was her affair. Americans were impossible, anyhow.

"How long have you been in the Orient?" Elsa asked.

"Ten years," he answered gravely.

"That is a long time."

"Sometimes it was like eternity."

"I have heard from the purser of your good luck."

"Oh!" He stooped again and locked the door of Rajah's cage. "I dare say a good many people will hear of it."

"It was splendid. I love to read stories like that, but I'd far rather hear them told first-hand."

Elsa was not romantic in the sense that she saw heroes where there were only ordinary men; but she thrilled at the telling of some actual adventure,

44

something big with life. Her heart and good will went out to the man who won against odds. Strangely enough, soldier's daughter though she was, the pomp and glamour and cruelty of war were detestable to her. It was the obscure and unknown hero who appealed to her: such a one as this man might be.

"Oh, there was nothing splendid about the thing. I simply hung on." Then a thought struck him. "You are traveling alone?"

"With a companion." A peculiar question, she thought.

"It is not wise," he commented.

"My father was a soldier," she replied.

"It isn't a question of bravery," he replied, a bit of color charging under his skin.

Elsa was amused. "And, pray, what question is it?" He was like a boy.

"I'm afraid of making myself obscure. This world is not like your world. Women over here. . . . Oh, I've lost the art of saying things clearly." He pulled at his beard embarrassedly.

"I rather believe I understand you. The veneer cracks easily in hot climates; man's veneer."

45

"And falls off altogether."

" Are you warning me against yourself? "

" Why not? Twenty thousand pounds do not change a man; they merely change the public's opinion of him. For all you know, I may be the greatest rascal unhanged."

" But you are not."

He recognized that it was not a query; and a pleasurable thrill ran over him. Had there been the least touch of condescension in her manner, he would have gone deep into his shell.

" No; there are worse men in this world than I. But we are getting away from the point, of women traveling alone in the East. Oh, I know you can protect yourself to a certain extent. But everywhere, on boats, in the hotels, on the streets, are men who have discarded all the laws of convention, of the social contract. And they have the keen eye of the kite and the vulture."

To Elsa this interest in her welfare was very diverting. " In other words, they can quickly discover the young woman who goes about unprotected? Don't you think that the trend of the con-

46

versation has taken rather a remarkable turn, not as impersonal as it should be?"

"I beg your pardon!"

"I am neither an infant nor a fool, Mr. Warrington."

"Shall I go?"

"No. I want you to tell me some stories." She laughed. "Don't worry about me, Mr. Warrington. I have gone my way alone since I was sixteen. I have traveled all over this wicked world with nobody but the woman who was once my nurse. I seldom put myself in the way of an affront. I am curious without being of an investigating turn of mind. Now, tell me something of your adventures. Ten years in this land must mean something. I am always hunting for Harun-al-Raschid, or Sindbad, or some one who has done something out of the ordinary."

"Do you write books?"

"No, I read them by preference."

"Ah, a good book!" He inclined against the rail and stared down at the muddy water. "Adventure?" He frowned a little. "I'm afraid

47

mine wouldn't read like adventures. There's no glory in being a stevedore on the docks at Hongkong, a stoker on a tramp steamer between Singapore and the Andaman Islands. What haven't I been in these ten years?" with a shrug. "Can you fancy me a deck-steward on a P. & O. boat, tucking old ladies in their chairs, staggering about with a tray of broth-bowls, helping the unsteady to their staterooms, and touching my cap at the end of the voyage for a few shillings in tips?"

"You are bitter."

"Bitter? I ought not to be, with twenty thousand pounds in my pocket."

"Tell me more."

He looked into her beautiful face, animated by genuine interest, and wondered if all men were willing so readily to obey her.

"It always interests me to hear from the man's own lips how he overcame obstacles."

"Sometimes I didn't overcome them. I ran away. After all, the strike in oil was a fluke."

"I don't think so. But go on," she prompted.

"Well, I've been manager of a cocoanut plantation in Penang; I've helped lay tracks in Upper

THE WEAK LINK

India; had a hand in some bridges; sold patent-medicines; worked in a ruby mine; been a haberdasher in the Whiteaway, Laidlaw shop in Bombay; cut wood in the teak forests; helped exterminate the plague at Chitor and Udaipur; and never saved a penny. I never had an adventure in all my life."

" Why, your wanderings were adventures," she insisted. " Think of the things you could tell! "

" And never will," a smile breaking over his face.

How like Arthur's that smile was! thought the girl. " Romantic persons never have any adventures. It is to the prosaic these things fall. Because of their nearness you lose their values."

" There is some difference between romance and adventure. Romance is what you look forward to; adventure is something you look back upon. If many disagreeable occupations, hunger and an occasional fisticuff, may be classed as adventure, then I have had my run of it. But I always supposed adventure was the finding of treasures, on land and on sea; of filibustering; of fighting with sabers and pistols, and all that rigmarole. I can't quite lift my imagination up to the height of calling my six months' shovel-engineering on *The Galle* an adventure. It was brutal hard work; and many times I wanted to jump over. The Lascars often got out of trouble that way."

"It all depends upon how we look at things." She touched the parrot-cage with her foot, and Rajah hissed. "What would you say if I told you that I was unconventional enough to ask the purser to introduce you?"

The amazement in his face was answer enough.

"Don't you suppose," she went on, "the picture you presented, standing on that ledge, the red light of the torch on your face, the bird-cage in your hand,— don't you suppose you roused my sense of the romantic to the highest pitch? Parrot & Co.!" with a wave of her hands.

She was laughing at him. It could not be otherwise. It made him at once sad and angry. "Romance! I hate the word. Once I was as full of romance as a water-chestnut is of starch. I again affirm that young women should not travel alone. They think every bit of tinsel is gold, every bit of colored glass, ruby. Go home; don't bother about romance outside of books. There it is safe. The English are right. They may be snobs when they travel abroad, but they travel securely. Romance, adventure! Bah! So much twaddle has been written about the East that cads and scoundrels are mistaken for Galahads and D'Artagnans. Few men remain in this country who can with honor leave it. Who knows what manner of man I am?"

He picked up the parrot-cage and strode away.

" Jah, jah!" began the bird.

Not all the diplomacy which worldly-wise men have at their disposal could have drawn this girl's interest more surely than the abrupt rude manner of his departure.

IV

A T first Elsa did not know whether she was annoyed or amused. The man's action was absurd, or would have been in any other man. There was something so singularly boyish in his haste that she realized she could not deal with him in an ordinary fashion. She ought to be angry; indeed, she wanted to be very angry with him; but her lips curled, and laughter hung upon them, undecided. His advice to her to go home was downright impudence; and yet, the sight of the parrot-cage, dangling at his side, made it impossible for her to take lasting offense. Once upon a time there had been a little boy who played in her garden. When he was cross he would take his playthings and go home. The boy might easily have been this man Warrington, grown up.

Of course he would come and apologize to her for his rudeness. That was one of the necessary laws of convention; and ten years spent in jungles and deserts and upon southern seas could not possibly have robbed him of the memory of these simple ethics that he had observed in other and better times. Perhaps he had resented her curiosity; perhaps her questions had been pressed too hard; and perhaps he had suddenly doubted her genuine interest. At any rate, it was a novel experience. And that bewildering likeness!

She returned to her chair and opened the book again. And as she read her wonder grew. How trivial it was, after all. The men and women she had calmly and even gratefully accepted as types were nothing more than marionettes, which the author behind the booth manipulated not badly but perfunctorily. The diction was exquisite; there was style; but now as she read there was lacking the one thing that stood for life, blood. It did not pulsate in the veins of these people. Until now she had not recognized this fact, and she was half-way through the book. She even took the trouble to re-read the chapter she had thought peculiarly effective. There was the same lack of feeling. What had happened to her since yesterday? To what

cause might be assigned this opposite angle of vision, so clearly defined?

The book fell upon her knees, and dreamily she watched the perspective open and divaricate. Full in her face the south wind blew, now warmed by the sun and perfumed by unknown spices. She took in little sharp breaths, but always the essence escaped her. The low banks with their golden haze of dust, the cloudless sky, the sad and lonely white pagodas, charmed her; and the languor of the East crept stealthily into her northern blood. She was not conscious of the subtle change; she only knew that the world of yesterday was unlike that of to-day.

Warrington, after depositing Rajah in the stateroom, sought the bench on the stern-deck. He filled his cutty with purser-loaned tobacco, and roundly damned himself as a blockhead. He had forgotten all the niceties of civilization; he no longer knew how to behave. What if she had been curious? It was natural that she should be. This was a strange world to her, and if her youth rosaltinted it with romance, what right had he to disillusion her? The first young woman in all these years who had treated him as an equal, and he had straightway proceeded to lecture her upon the evils of traveling alone in the Orient! Double-dyed ass! He had been rude and impudent. He had seen other women traveling alone, but the sight had not roused him as in the present instance. In ten years he had not said so much to all the women he had met; and without seeming effort at all she had dragged forth some of the half-lights of his past. This in itself amazed him; it proved that he was still weak enough to hunger for human sympathy, and he of all men deserved none whatever. He had been a fool as a boy, a fool as a man, and without doubt he would die a fool. He was of half a mind to leave the boat at Prome and take the train down to Rangoon.

And yet he had told her the truth. It was not right that a young and attractive woman should wander about in the East, unattended save by a middle-aged companion. It would provoke the devil in men who were not wholly bad. Women had the fallible idea that they could read human nature, and never found out their mistake until after they were married. He knew her kind. If she

55

wanted to walk through the bazaars in the evening, she would do so. If a man followed her she would ignore the fact. If he caught up with her and spoke, she would continue on as if she had not heard. If a man touched her, she would rely upon the fire of her eyes. She would never call out for help. Some women were just that silly.

He bit hard upon the stem of his pipe. What was all this to him? Why should he bother his head about a woman he had known but a few hours? Ah, why lie to himself? He knew what Elsa, usually quick and receptive, did not know, that he was not afraid of her, but terribly afraid of himself. For things ripen quickly in the East, men and women, souls and deeds. And he was something like the pariah-dog; spoken kindly to, it attached itself immediately and enduringly.

He struck the cutty against his boot-heel. Why not? It would be only for two days. At Rangoon their paths would separate; he would never see her again. He got up. He would go to her at once and apologize abjectly. And thus he surrendered to the very devil he had but a moment gone so vigorously discountenanced.

TWO DAYS OF PARADISE

He found her asleep in her chair. The devil which had brought him to her side was thrust back. Why, she was nothing more than a beautiful child! A great yearning to brother her came into his heart. He did not disturb her, but waited until five, that grave and sober hour, when kings and clerks stop work for no logical reason whatever — tea. She opened her eyes and saw him watching her. He rose quickly.

"May I get you some tea?"

"Thank you."

And so the gulf was bridged. When he returned he set the cup and plate of cakes on the arm of her chair.

"I was very rude a little while ago. Will you accept my apologies?"

"On condition that you will never take your playthings and go home."

He laughed engagingly. "You've hit it squarely. It was the act of a petulant child."

"It did not sound exactly like a man who had stoked six months from Singapore to the Andaman Islands. But there is one thing I must understand before this acquaintance continues. You said,

'Who knows what manner of man I am?' Have you ever done anything that would conscientiously forbid you to speak to a young unmarried woman?"

Take care of herself? He rather believed she could. The bluntness of her question dissipated any doubt that remained.

"No. I haven't been that kind of a man," simply. "I could look into my mother's eyes without any sense of shame, if that is what you mean."

"That is all I care to know. Your mother is living?"

"Yes. But I haven't seen her in ten years." His mother! His brows met in a frown. His proud beautiful mother!

Elsa saw the frown, and realized that she had approached delicate ground. She stirred her tea and sipped it slowly.

"There has been a deal of chatter about shifty untrustworthy eyes," he said. "The greatest liars I have ever known could look St. Peter straight and serenely in the eye. It's a matter of steady nerves, nothing more. Somebody says that so and so is a fact, and we go on believing it for years, until some one who is not a person but an individual explodes it."

" I agree with you. But there is something we rely upon far more than either eyes or ears, instinct. It is that attribute of the animal which civilization has not yet successfully dulled. Women rely upon that more readily than men."

" And make more mistakes," with a cynicism he could not conceal.

She had no ready counter for this. " Do you go home from Rangoon, now that you have made your fortune? "

" No. I am going to Singapore. I shall make my plans there."

Singapore. Elsa stirred uneasily. It would be like having a ghost by her side. She wanted to tell him what had really drawn her interest. But it seemed to her that the moment to do so had passed.

" Vultures! How I detest them! " She pointed toward a sand-bar upon which stood several of these abominable birds and an adjutant, solemn and aloof.

"At Lucknow they were red-headed. I do not recollect seeing one of them fly. But I admire the kites; they look so much like our eagles."

"And thus again the eye misleads us. There is nothing that flies so rapacious as the kite."

Little by little she drew from him a sketch here, a phase there. She was given glimpses into the life of the East such as no book or guide had ever given; and the boat was circling toward the landing at Prome before they became aware of the time.

Warrington rushed ashore to find the dry-goods shop. His social redemption was on the way, if vanity went for anything. It was stirring and tingling with life again. With the money advanced by the purser he bought shirts and collars and ties; and as he possessed no watch, returned barely in time to dress for dinner. He was not at all disturbed to learn that the inquisitive German, the colonel and his fidgety charges, had decided to proceed to Rangoon by rail. Indeed, there was a bit of exultation in his manner as he observed the vacant chairs. Paradise for two whole days. And he proposed to make the most of it. Now, his mind was as clear of evil as a forest spring. He simply wanted to play; wanted to give rein to the lighter emotions so long pent up in his lonely heart.

The purser, used to these sudden changes and desertions in his passenger-lists, gave the situation no thought. But Elsa saw a mild danger, all the more alluring because it hung nebulously. For years she had walked in conformity with the cramped and puerile laws that govern society. She had obeyed most of them from habit, others from necessity. What harm could there be in having a little fling? He was so amazingly like outwardly, so astonishingly unlike inwardly, that the situation held for her a subtle fascination against which she was in nowise inclined to fight. What had nature in mind when she produced two men exactly alike in appearance but in reality as far apart as the poles? Would it be worth while to find out? She was not wholly ignorant of her power. She could bend the man if she tried. Should she try?

They were like two children, setting out to play a game with fire.

She thought of Arthur. Had he gone the length of his thirty-five years without his peccadillos? Scarcely. She understood the general run of men well enough to accept this fact. Whomever she married she was never going to worry him with questions regarding his bachelor life. Nor did she propose to be questioned about her own past. Besides, she hadn't married Arthur yet; she had only promised to. And such promises were sometimes sensibly broken. There ran through her a fine vein of mercilessness, but it was without cruelty, it was leavened with both logic and justice. When the time came she would name the day to Arthur, or she would with equal frankness announce that she would not marry him at all. These thoughts flashed through her mind, disconnectedly, while she talked and laughed.

It never occurred to her to have Martha moved up from the foot of the table. Once or twice she stole a glance at the woman who had in the olden days dandled her on her knees. The glance was a mixture of guilt and mischief, like a child's. But the glance had not the power to attract Martha's eyes. Martha felt the glances as surely as if she had lifted her eyes to meet them. She held her peace. She had not been brought along as Elsa's guardian. Elsa was not self-willed but strong-willed, and Martha realized that any interference would result in estrangement. In fact, Martha beheld in Warrington a real menace. The extraordinary resemblance would naturally appeal to Elsa, with what results she could only imagine. Later she asked Elsa if she had told Warrington of the remarkable resemblance.

" Mercy, no! And what is more, I do not want him to know. Men are vain as a rule; and I should not like to hurt his vanity by telling him that I sought his acquaintance simply because he might easily have been Arthur Ellison's twin brother."

" The man you are engaged to marry."

" Whom I have promised to marry, provided the state of my sentiments is unchanged upon my return; which is altogether a different thing."

" That does not seem quite fair to Mr. Ellison."

" Well, Martha? "

" I beg your pardon, Elsa; but the stranger terrifies me. He is something uncanny."

" Nonsense! You've been reading tales about Yogii."

" It is a terrible country."

" It is the East, Martha, the East. Here a man

63

may wear a dress-suit and a bowler without offend-
ing any one."

"And a woman may talk to any one she pleases."

"Is that a criticism?"

"No, Elsa; it is what you call the East."

"You have been with me twenty years," began
Elsa coldly.

"And love you better than the whole world!
And I wish I could guard you always from harm
and evil. Those horrid old Englishwomen . . ."

"Oh; so there's been gossip already? You
know my views regarding gossip. So long as I
know that I am doing no wrong, ladies may gossip
their heads off. I'm not a kitten."

"You are twenty-five, and yet you're only a
child."

"What does that signify? That I am too young
to manage my own affairs? That I must set my
clock as others order? Good soul!" putting her
arms around the older woman. "Don't worry
about Elsa Chetwood. Her life is her own, but
she will never misuse it."

"Oh, if you were only married and settled
down!"

TWO DAYS OF PARADISE

"You mean, if I were happily married and settled down. There you have it. I'm in search of happiness. That's the Valley of Diamonds. When I find that, Martha, you may fold your hands in peace."

"Grant it may be soon! I hate the East!"

"And I have just begun to love it."

V

BACK TO LIFE

THE two days between Prome and Rangoon were distinctly memorable for the subtle changes wrought in the man and woman. Those graces of mind and manner which had once been the man's, began to find expression. Physically, his voice became soft and mellow; his hands became full of emphasis; his body grew less and less clumsy, more and more leonine. It has taken centuries and centuries to make the white man what he is to-day; yet, a single year of misfortune may throw him back into the primordial. For it is far easier to retrograde than to go forward, easier to let the world go by than to march along with it. Had he been less interested in Elsa and more concerned about his rehabilitation, self-analysis would have astonished Warrington. The blunt speech, the irritability in argument, the stupid pauses, the painful study of cunning phrases, the suspicion and reticence that figuratively encrust the hearts of shy and lonely men, these vanished under her warm if careless glances. For the first time in ten years a woman of the right sort was showing interest in him. True, there had been other women, but these had served only to make him retreat farther into his shell.

If the crust of barbarism is thick, that of civilization is thin enough. As Warrington went forward, Elsa stopped, and gradually went back, not far, but far enough to cause her to throw down the bars of reserve, to cease to guard her impulses against the invasion of interest and fascination. She faced the truth squarely, without palter. The man fascinated her. He was like a portrait with following eyes. She spoke familiarly of her affairs (always omitting Arthur); she talked of her travels, of the famous people she had met, of the wonderful pageants she had witnessed. And she secretly laughed at reproachful conscience that urged her to recall one of those laws Elsa herself had written down to follow: that which forbade a young unmarried woman to seek the companionship of a man about whom she knew nothing. It was not her fault that, with the exception of Martha who didn't count, they two were the only passengers. This condition of affairs was directly chargeable to fate; and before the boat reached Rangoon, Elsa was quite willing to let fate shift and set the scenes how it would. The first step toward reversion is the casting aside of one's responsibilities. Elsa shifted her cares to the shoulders of fate. So long as the man behaved himself, so long as he treated her with respect, real or feigned, nothing else mattered.

The phase that escaped her entirely was this, that had he not progressed, she would have retained her old poise, the old poise of which she was never again to be mistress. It is the old tale: sympathy to lift up another first steps down. And never had her sympathy gone out so quickly to any mortal. Elsa had a horror of loneliness, and this man seemed to be the living presentment of the word. What struggles, and how simply he recounted them! What things he had seen, what adventures had befallen him, what romance and mystery! She wondered if there had been a woman in his life and if she had been the cause of his downfall. Every day of the

past ten years lay open for her to admire or condemn, but beyond these ten years there was a
Chinese Wall, over which she might not look. Only
once had she provoked the silent negative nod of his
head. He was strong. Not the smallest corner of
the veil was she permitted to turn aside. She
walked hither and thither along the scarps and bas-
tions of the barrier, but never found the breach.

" Will you come and dine with me to-night? " she
asked, as they left the boat.

" No, Miss Innocence."

" That's silly. There isn't a soul I know here."

" But," gravely he replied, " there are many here
who know me."

" Which infers that my invitation is unwise? "

" Absolutely unwise."

" Tea? "

" Frankly, I ought not to be seen with you."

" Why? Unless, indeed, you have not told me
the truth."

" I have told you the truth."

" Then where's the harm? "

" For myself, none. On the boat it did not matter so much. It was a situation which neither of

us could foresee nor prevent. I have told you that people here look askance at me because they know nothing about me, save that I came from the States. And they are wise. I should be a cad if I accepted your invitation to dinner."

" Then, I am not to see you again? "

The smile would have lured him across three continents. " To-morrow, I promise to call and have tea with you, much against my better judgment."

" Oh, if you don't want to come . . ."

" Don't want to come! "

Something in his eyes caused Elsa to speak hurriedly. " Good-by until to-morrow."

She gave him her hand for a moment, stepped into the carriage, which already held Martha and the luggage, and then drove off to the Strand Hotel.

He stood with his helmet in his hand. A fine warm rain was falling, but he was not conscious of it. It seemed incredible that time should produce such a change within the space of seventy hours, a little more, a little less. As she turned and waved a friendly hand, he knew that the desolation which had been his for ten years was nothing as compared to that which now fell upon his heart. She was as unattainable as the north star; and nothing, time nor circumstance, could bridge that incalculable distance. She was the most exquisite contradiction; in one moment the guilelessness of a child, in another, the worldly-wise woman. Had she been all of the one or all of the other, he would not have been touched so deeply. If she loved a man, there would be no silly doddering; the voice of the petty laws that strove to hedge her in would be in her ears as a summer breeze. For one so young — and twenty-five was young — she possessed a disconcerting directness in her logic. So far he observed that she retained but one illusion, that somewhere in the world there was a man worth loving. His heart hurt him. He must see her no more after the morrow. Enchantment and happiness were two words which fate had ruthlessly scratched from his book of days.

Mr. Hooghly had already started off toward the town, the kit-bag and the valise slung across his shoulders, the parrot-cage bobbing at his side. He knew where to go; an obscure lodging for men in the heart of the business section, known in jest by the derelicts as The Stranded.

Warrington, becoming suddenly aware that his pose, if prolonged, would become ridiculous, put on his helmet and proceeded to the Bank of Burma. To-day was Wednesday; Thursday week he would sail for Singapore and close the chapter. Before banking hours were over, his financial affairs were put in order, and he walked forth with two letters of credit and enough bank-notes and gold to carry him around the world, if so he planned. Next, he visited a pawn-shop and laid down a dozen mutilated tickets, receiving in return a handsome watch, emerald cuff-buttons, some stick-pins, some pearls, and a beautiful old ruby ring, a gift of the young Maharajah of Udaipur. The ancient Chinaman smiled. This was a rare occasion. Men generally went out of his dark and dingy shop and never more returned.

" Much money. Can do now? " affably.

" Can do," replied Warrington, slipping the treasures into a pocket. What a struggle it had been to hold them! Somehow or other he had always been able to meet the interest; though, often to accomplish this feat he had been forced to go without tobacco for weeks.

There is a vein of superstition in all of us, deny it how we will. Certain inconsequent things we do or avoid doing. We never walk home on the opposite side of the street. We carry luck-stones and battered pieces of copper that have ceased to serve as coins. We fill the garret with useless junk. Warrington was as certain of the fact as he was of the rising and the setting of the sun, that if he lost these heirlooms, he never could go back to the old familiar world, the world in which he had moved and lived and known happiness. Never again would he part with them. A hundred thousand dollars, almost; with his simple wants he was now a rich man.

" Buy ling? " asked the Chinaman. He rolled a mandarin's ring carelessly across the show-case. " Gold; all heavy; velly old, velly good ling."

" What does it say? " asked Warrington, pointing to the characters.

" Good luck and plospeity; velly good signs."

It was an unusually beautiful ring, unusual in that it had no setting of jade. Warrington offered three sovereigns for it. The Chinaman smiled and put the ring away. Warrington laughed and laid down five pieces of gold. The Chinaman swept them up in his lean dry hands. And Warrington departed, wondering if she would accept such a token.

By four o'clock he arrived at the Chinese tailors in the Suley Pagoda Road. He ordered a suit of pongee, to be done at noon the following day. He added to this orders for four other suits, to be finished within a week. Then he went to the shoemaker, to the hatter, to the haberdasher. There was even a light Malacca walking-stick among his purchases. A long time had passed since he had carried a cane. There used to be, once upon a time, a dapper light bamboo which was known up and down Broadway, in the restaurants, the more or less famous bars, and in the lounging-rooms of a popular club. All this business because he wanted her to realize what he had been and yet could be. Thus, vanity sometimes works out a man's salvation. And it marked the end of Warrington's recidivation.

When he reached his lodging-house he sought

the Burmese landlady. She greeted him with a smile and a stiff little shake of the hand. He owed her money, but that was nothing. Had he not sent her drunken European sailor-man husband about his business? Had he not freed her from a tyranny of fists and curses? It had not affected her in the least to learn that her sailor-man had been negligently married all the way from Yokohama to Colombo. She was free of him.

Warrington spread out a five-pound note and laid ten sovereigns upon it. "There we are," he said genially; "all paid up to date."

"This?" touching the note.

"A gift for all your patience and kindness."

"You go 'way?" the smile leaving her pretty moon-face.

"Yes."

"You like?" with a gesture which indicated the parlor and its contents. "Be boss? Half an' half?"

He shook his head soberly. She picked up the money and jingled it in her hand.

"Goo'-by!" softly.

"Oh, I'm not going until next Thursday."

The smile returned to her face, and her body bent in a kind of kotow. He was so big, and his beard glistened like the gold-leaf on the Shwe Dagon Pagoda. She understood. The white to the white and the brown to the brown; it was the Law.

Warrington went up to his room. He was welcomed by a screech from the parrot and a dignified salaam from James, who was trimming the wick of the oil-lamp. For the last year and a half this room had served as headquarters. Many a financial puzzle had been pieced together within these dull drab walls; many a dream had gone up to the ceiling, only to sink and dissipate like smoke. There were no pictures on the walls, no photographs. In one corner, on the floor, was a stack of dilapidated books. These were mostly old novels and tomes dealing with geological and mathematical matters; laughter and tears and adventure, sandwiched in between the dry positiveness of straight lines and squares and circles and numerals without end; D'Artagnan hobnobbing with Euclid! Warrington was an educated man, but he was in no sense a scholar. In his hours of leisure he did not find solace in the classics. He craved for a good blood-red tale, with lots of fighting and love-making and pleasant endings.

James applied a match to the wick, and the general poverty of the room was instantly made manifest.

" Well, old sober-top, suppose we square up and part like good friends? "

" I am always the Sahib's good friend."

" Right as rain! " Warrington emptied his pockets upon the table; silver and gold and paper. " Eh? That's the stuff. Without it the world's not worth a tinker's dam. Count out seventy pounds, James."

" Sixty-seven."

" Seventy or nothing," declared Warrington, putting his hands down upon the glittering metals. Rupees and sovereigns never lose their luster in the East.

Calmly, then, James took sovereign after sovereign until he had withdrawn the required sum. " Gold is heavy, Sahib," he commented.

" Hang it, your hands are steadier than mine! "

" You go back home? "

"Yes. Something like home. I am going to Paris, where good people go when they die. I am going to drink vintage wines, eat truffles and mushrooms and caviar, and kiss the pretty girls in Maxim's. I've been in prison for ten years. I am free, free!" Warrington flung out his arms. "Good-by, jungles, deserts, hell-heat and thirsty winds! Good-by, crusts and rags and hunger! I am going to live."

"The Sahib has fever," observed the unimaginative Eurasian.

"That's the word; fever. I am burning up. Here; go to the boat and give the purser these six sovereigns. Here are three more. Go to the Strand and get a bottle of champagne, and bring some ice. Buy a box of the best cigars, and hurry back. Then put this junk in the trunk. And damn the smell of kerosene!"

James raised his hand warningly. From the adjoining room came the sound of a quarrel.

"Rupees one hundred and forty, and I want it now, you sneak!"

"But I told you I couldn't square up until the first of the month."

" You had no business to play poker, then, if you knew you couldn't settle."

" Who asked me to play? " shrilled the other.
" You did. Well, I haven't got the money."

" You miserable little welcher! That ring is worth a hundred and forty."

" You'll never get your dirty fingers inside of that."

" Oh, I shan't, eh?"

Warrington heard a scuffling, which was presently followed by a low choking sob. He did not know who occupied the adjoining room. He had been away for weeks, and there had been no permanent boarders before that time. He rushed fearlessly into the other room. Pinned to the wall was a young man with a weak pale face. The other man presented nothing more than the back of his broad muscular shoulders. The disparity in weight and height was sufficient to rouse Warrington's sense of fair play. Besides, he was in a rough mood himself.

" Here, that'll do," he cried, seizing the heavier man by the collar. " It isn't worth while to kill a man for a handful of rupees. Let go, you fool!"

He used his strength. The man and his victim swung in a half-circle and crashed to the floor.

With a snarl and an oath, the gambler sprung to his feet and started toward Warrington. He stopped short.

" Good God! " he murmured; and retreated until he touched the foot-board of the bed.

VI

"CRAIG?" Warrington whispered the word, as if he feared the world might hear the deadly menace in his voice. For murder leaped up in his heart as flame leaps up in pine-kindling.

The weak young man got to his knees, then to his feet. He steadied himself by clutching the back of a chair. With one hand he felt of his throat tenderly.

"He tried to kill me, the blackguard!" he croaked.

"Craig, it *is* you! For ten years I've never thought of you without murder in my heart. Newell Craig, and here, right where I can put my hands upon you! Oh, this old world is small." Warrington laughed. It was a high thin sound.

The young man looked from his enemy to his deliverer, and back again. What new row was this? Never before had he seen the blackguard with that look in his dark, handsome, predatory face. It typified fear. And who was this big blond chap whose fingers were working so convulsively?

"Craig," said the young man, "you get out of here, and if you ever come bothering me, I'll shoot you. Hear me?"

This direful threat did not seem to stir the sense of hearing in either of the two men. The one faced the other as a lion might have faced a jackal, wondering if it would be worth while to waste a cuff on so sorry a beast. Suddenly the blond man caught the door and swung it wide.

"Craig, a week ago I'd have throttled you without the least compunction. To-day I can't touch you. But get out of here as fast as you can. You might have gone feet foremost. Go! Out of Rangoon, too. I may change my mind."

The man called Craig walked out, squaring his shoulders with a touch of bravado that did not impress even the plucked pigeon. Warrington stood listening until he heard the hall-door close sharply.

"Thanks," said the bewildered youth.

Warrington whirled upon him savagely.

IN THE NEXT ROOM

" Thanks? Don't thank me, you weak-kneed fool! "

" Oh, I say, now! " the other protested.

" Be silent! If you owe that scoundrel anything, refuse to pay it. He never won a penny in his life without cheating. Keep out of his way; keep out of the way of all men who prefer to deal only two hands." And with this advice Warrington stepped out into the hallway and shut the door rudely.

The youth walked over to the mirror and straightened his collar and tie. " Rum go, that. Narrow squeak. Surly beggar, even if he did do me a good turn. I shan't have to pay that rotter, Craig, now. That's something."

" Pay the purser and get a box of cigars," Warrington directed James. " Never mind about the wine. I shan't want it now."

James went out upon the errands immediately.

Warrington dropped down in the creaky rocking-chair, the only one in the boarding-house. He stared at the worn and faded carpet. How dingy everything looked! What a sordid rut he had been content to lie in! Chance: to throw this man across his path when he had almost forgotten him, forgotten that he had sworn to break the man's neck over his knees! In the very next room! And he had permitted him to go unharmed simply because his mind was full of a girl he would never see again after to-morrow. What was the rascal doing over here? What had caused him to forsake the easy pluckings of Broadway in exchange for a dog's life on packet-boats, in squalid boarding-houses like this one, and in dismal billiard-halls? Wire-tapper, racing-tout, stool-pigeon, a cheater at cards, blackmailer and trafficker in baser things; in the next room, and he had let him go unharmed. Vermin. Pah! He was glad. The very touch of the man's collar had left a sense of defilement upon his hands. Ten years ago and thirteen thousand miles away. In the next room. He laughed unpleasantly. Chivalric fool, silly Don Quixote, sentimental dreamer, to have made a hash of his life in this manner!

He leaned toward the window-sill and opened the cage. Rajah walked out, muttering.

When it was possible, Elsa preferred to walk. She was young and strong and active; and she went along with a swinging stride that made obvious a serene confidence in her ability to take care of herself. She was, in many respects, a remarkable young woman. She had been pampered, she had been given her head; and still she was unspoiled. What the unknowing called wilfulness was simply natural independence, which she asserted whenever occasion demanded it.

Tongas cut into her nerves, the stuffy gharry made her head ache, and the springless phaetons which abound in the East she avoided as the plague. Elephants and camels and rickshaws were her delight; but here in Rangoon none of these was available. There were no camels; the government elephants had steady employment out at MacGregor's timber-yards and could not get leave of absence; while rickshaws were out of fashion, as only natives and Chinamen rode in them. So Elsa walked.

She loved to prowl through the strange streets and alleys and stranger shops; it was a joy to ramble about, minus the irritating importunities of guide or attendant. It was great fun, but it was not always wise. There were some situations which only men could successfully handle. Elsa would never confess that there had been instances when she had been confronted by such situations. She could, however, truthfully say that these awkward moments had always been without endings, as, being an excellent runner, she had, upon these occasions, blithely taken to her heels.

In her cool white drill, her wide white pith-helmet, she presented a charming picture. The exercise had given her cheeks a bit of color, and her eyes sparkled and flashed like raindrops. This morning she had taken Martha along merely to still her protests.

"It's all right so long as we keep to the main streets," said the harried Martha; "but I do not like the idea of roaming about in the native quarters. This is not like Europe. The hotel-manager said we ought to have a man."

"He is looking out for his commission. Heavens! what is the matter with everybody? One would think, the way people put themselves out to warn you, that murder and robbery were daily occurrences in Asia. I've been here four months, and the only disagreeable moment I have known was caused by a white man."

86

IN THE NEXT ROOM

" Because we have been lucky so far, it's no sign that we shall continue so."

" Raven ! " laughed the girl.

Martha shut her lips grimly. Her worry was not confined to this particular phase of Elsa's imperious moods; it was general. There was that blond man with the parrot. Martha was beginning to see him in her dreams, which she considered as a presage of evil. There was also the astonishing lack of interest in the man who was waiting at home. Elsa rarely spoke of him. Nobody could tell Martha that chance had thrown the blond stranger into their society. Somewhere it had been written. (As, indeed, it had!) How to keep Elsa apart from him was now her vital concern. She would never feel at ease until they were out of Yokohama, homeward-bound.

" I feel like a child this morning," said Elsa. " I want to run and play and shout."

" All the more reason why you should have a guardian. . . . Look, Elsa ! " Martha caught the girl by the arm. " There's that man we left at Mandalay."

" Where? "

" Coming toward us. Shall we go into this shop? "

" No, thank you! There is no reason why I should hide in a butcher-shop, simply to avoid meeting the man. We'll walk straight past him. If he speaks, we'll ignore him."

" I wish we were in a civilized country."

" This man is supposed to be civilized. Don't let him catch your eye. Go on; don't lag."

Craig stepped in front of them, smiling as he raised his helmet. " This is an unexpected pleasure."

Elsa, looking coldly beyond him, attempted to pass.

" Surely you remember me? "

" I remember an insolent cad," replied Elsa, her eyes beginning to burn dangerously. " Will you stand aside? "

He threw a swift glance about. He saw with satisfaction that none but natives was in evidence.

Elsa's glance roved, too, with a little chill of despair. In stories Warrington would have appeared about this time and soundly trounced this impudent scoundrel. She realized that she must settle this affair alone. She was not a soldier's daughter for nothing.

" Stand aside! "

" Hoity-toity! " he laughed. He had been drinking liberally and was a shade reckless. " Why not be a good fellow? Over here nobody minds. I know a neat little restaurant. Bring the old lady along," with a genial nod toward the quaking Martha.

Resolutely Elsa's hand went up to her helmet, and with a flourish drew out one of the long steel pins.

" Oh, Elsa! " warned Martha.

" Be still! This fellow needs a lesson. Once more, Mr. Craig, will you stand aside? "

Had he been sober he would have seen the real danger in the young woman's eyes.

" Cruel! " he said. " At least, one kiss," putting out his arms.

Elsa, merciless in her fury, plunged the pin into his wrist. It stung like a hornet; and with a gasp of pain, Craig leaped back out of range, sobered.

" Why, you she-cat! "

" I warned you," she replied, her voice steady but

89

low. " The second stab will be serious. Stand aside."

He stepped into the gutter, biting his lips and straining his uninjured hand over the hurting throb in his wrist. The hat-pin as a weapon of defense he had hitherto accepted as reporters' yarns. He was now thoroughly convinced of the truth. He had had wide experience with women. His advantage had always been in the fact that the general run of them will submit to insult rather than create a scene. This dark-eyed Judith was distinctly an exception to the rule. Gad! She might have missed his wrist and jabbed him in the throat. He swore, and walked off down the street.

Elsa set a pace which Martha, with her wabbling knees, found difficult to maintain.

" You might have killed him! " she cried breathlessly.

" You can't kill that kind of a snake with a hatpin; you have to stamp on its head. But I rather believe it will be some time before Mr. Craig will again make the mistake of insulting a woman because she appears to be defenseless." Elsa's chin was in the air. The choking sensation in her throat began to subside. "The deadly hat-pin; can't you see the story in the newspapers? Well, I for one am not afraid to use it. You know and the purser knows what happened on the boat to Mandalay. He was plausible and affable and good-looking, and the mistake was mine. I seldom make them. I kept quiet because the boat was full-up, and as a rule I hate scenes. Men like that know it. If I had complained, he would have denied his actions, inferred that I was evil-minded. He would have been shocked at my misinterpreting him. Heavens, I know the breed! Now, not a single word of this to any one. Mr. Craig, I fancy, will be the last person to speak of it."

"You had better put the pin back into your hat," suggested Martha.

"Pah! I had forgotten it." Elsa flung the weapon far into the street.

Once they turned into Merchant Street, both felt the tension relax. Martha would have liked to sit down, even on the curb.

"I despise men," she volunteered.

" I am beginning to believe that few of them are worth a thought. Those who aren't fools are knaves."

" Are you sure of your judgment in regard to this man Warrington? How can you tell that he is any different from that man Craig? "

" He is different, that is all. This afternoon he will come to tea. I shall want you to be with us. Remember, not a word of this disgraceful affair."

" Ah, Elsa, I am afraid; I am more afraid of Warrington than of a man of Craig's type."

" And why? "

" It sounds foolish, but I can't explain. I am just afraid of him."

" Bother! You talk like an old maid."

" And I am one, by preference."

" We are always quarreling, Martha; and it doesn't do either of us any good. When you oppose me, I find that that is the very thing I want to do. You haven't any diplomacy."

" I would gladly cultivate it if I thought it would prove effectual," was the retort.

" Try it," advised Elsa dryly.

Warrington's appearance that afternoon astonished Elsa. She had naturally expected some change, but scarcely such elegance. He was, without question, one of the handsomest men she had ever met. He was handsomer than Arthur because he was more manly in type. Arthur himself, an exquisite in the matter of clothes, could not have improved upon this man's taste or selection. What a mystery he was! She greeted him cordially, without restraint; but for all that, a little shiver stirred the tendrils of hair at the nape of her neck.

" The most famous man in Rangoon to-day," she said, smiling.

" So you have read that tommy-rot in the newspaper? "

They sat on her private balcony, under an awning. Rain was threatening. Martha laid aside her knitting and did her utmost to give her smile of welcome an air of graciousness.

" I shouldn't call it tommy-rot," Elsa declared. " It was not chance. It was pluck and foresight. Men who possess those two attributes get about everything worth having."

" There are exceptions," studying the ferrule of his cane.

" Is there really anything you want now and can't have ? "

Martha looked at her charge in dread and wonder.

" There is the moon," he answered. " I have always wanted that. But there it hangs, just as far out of reach as ever."

" Two lumps ? "

" None. My sugar-tooth is gone."

Elsa had heard that hard drinkers disliked sweets. Had this been the Gordian knot he had cut?

" Perhaps, after all," she said, " you would prefer a peg, as you call it over here."

" No, thanks. I was never fond of whisky. Sometimes, when I am dead tired, and have to go on working, I take a little."

So that wasn't it. Elsa's curiosity to-day was keenly alive. She wanted to ask a thousand questions ; but the ease with which the man wore his new clothes, used his voice and eyes and hands, convinced her more than ever that the subtlest questions she might devise would not stir him into any confession. That he had once been a gentleman of her own class, and more, something of an exquisite, there remained no doubt in her mind. What had he done? What in the world had he done?

On his part he regretted the presence of Martha; for, so strongly had this girl worked upon his imagination that he had called with the deliberate intention of telling her everything. But he could not open the gates of his heart before a third person, one he intuitively knew was antagonistic.

Conversation went afield: pictures and music and the polished capitals of the world; the latest books and plays. The information in regard to these Elsa supplied him. They discussed also the problems of the day as frankly as if they had been in an Occidental drawing-room. Martha's tea was bitter. She liked Arthur, who was always charming, who never surprised or astonished anybody, or shocked them with unexpected phases of character; and each time she looked at Warrington, Arthur seemed to recede. And when the time came for the guest to take his leave, Martha regretted to find that the major part of her antagonism was gone.

" I wish to thank you, Miss Chetwood, for your kindness to a very lonely man. It isn't probable that I shall see you again. I sail next Thursday for

Singapore." He reached into a pocket. "I wonder if you would consider it an impertinence if I offered you this old trinket?" He held out the mandarin's ring.

"What a beauty!" she exclaimed. "Of course I'll accept it. It is very kind of you. I am inordinately fond of such things. Thank you. How easily it slips over my finger!"

"Chinamen have very slender fingers," he explained. "Good-by. Those characters say 'Good luck and prosperity.'"

No expressed desire of wishing to meet her again; just an ordinary every-day farewell; and she liked him all the better for his apparent lack of sentiment.

"Good-by," she said. She winced, for his hand was rough-palmed and strong.

A little later she saw him pass down the street. He never turned and looked back.

"And why," asked Martha, "did you not tell the man that we sail on the same ship?"

"You're a simpleton, Martha." Elsa turned the ring round and round on her finger. "If I had told him, he would have canceled his sailing and taken another boat."

VII

THAT night Martha wrote a letter. During the writing of it she jumped at every sound: a footstep in the hall, the shutting of a door, a voice calling in the street. And yet, Martha was guilty of performing only what she considered to be her bounden duty. It is the prerogative of fate to tangle or untangle the skein of human lives; but still, there are those who elect themselves to break the news gently, to lessen the shock of the blow which fate is about to deliver.

"My dear Mr. Arthur:
. . . I do not know what to make of it. His likeness to you is the most unheard of thing. He is a little bigger and broader and he wears his beard longer. That's all the difference. When he came on the boat that night, it was like a hand clutching at my throat. And you know how romantic Elsa is, for all that she believes she is prosaic. I am certain that she sees you in this stranger who calls himself Warrington. If only you had had the foresight to follow us, a sailing or two later! And now they'll be together for four or five days, down to Singapore. I don't

like it. There's something uncanny in the thing. What if she did forbid you to follow? There are some promises women like men to break. You should have followed.

Neither of us has the slightest idea what the man has done to exile himself in this horrible land for ten years. He still behaves like a gentleman, and he must have been one in the past. But he has never yet spoken of his home, of his past, of his people. We don't even know that Warrington is his name. And you know that's a sign that something is wrong. I wonder if you have any relatives by the name of Warrington? I begin to see that man's face in my dreams.

I am worried. For Elsa is a puzzle. She has always been one to me. I have been with her since her babyhood, and yet I know as little of what goes on in her mind as a stranger would. Her father, you know, was a soldier, of fierce loves and hates; her mother was a handsome statue. Elsa has her father's scorn for convention and his independence, clothed in her mother's impenetrable mask. Don't mistake me. Elsa is the most adorable creature to me, and I worship her; but I worry about her. I believe that it would be wise on your part to meet us in San Francisco. Give my love and respect to your dear beautiful mother. And marry Elsa as fast as ever you can."

There followed some rambling comments on the weather, the rains and the dust, the execrable food and the lack of drinking-water. The man who eventually received this letter never reached that part of it.

The day of sailing was brilliant and warm. Elsa sat in a chair on the deck of the tender, watching the

CONFIDENCES

passengers as they came aboard. A large tourist party bustled about, rummaged among the heaps of luggage, and shouted questions at their unhappy conductor. They wanted to know where their staterooms were, grumbled about the size of the boat, prophesied typhoons and wrecks, got in everybody's way, and ordered other people's servants about. Never before had Elsa realized the difficulties that beset the path of the personal conductor. Whatever his salary was, he was entitled to it. It was all he got. No one thought to offer him a little kindness. He was a human guide-book which his fares opened and shut how and when they pleased.

She saw Hooghly standing in the bow. A steamer-trunk, a kit-bag, a bedding-bag, and the inevitable parrot-cage, reposed at his feet. He was watching without interest or excitement the stream passing up and down the gangplank. If his master came, very well; if he did not, he would get off with the luggage. How she would have liked to question him regarding his master! Elsa began to offer excuses for her interest in Warrington. He was the counterpart of Arthur Ellison. He had made his fortune against odds. He was a mystery.

PARROT & CO.

Why shouldn't he interest her? Her mind was not
ice, nor was her heart a stone. She pitied him,
always wondering what was back of it all. She
would be a week in Singapore; after that their paths
would widen and become lost in the future, and
she would forget all about him, save in a shadowy
way. She would marry Arthur whether she loved
him or not. She was certain that he loved her. He
had a comfortable income, not equal to hers, but
enough. He was, besides, her own sort; and there
wasn't any mystery about him at all. He was as
clear to her as glass. For nearly ten years she had
known him, since his and his mother's arrival in the
small pretty Kentuckian town. What was the use
of hunting a fancy? Yes, she would marry Arthur. She was almost inclined to cable him to meet
her in San Francisco.

That there was real danger in her interest in Warrington did not occur to her. The fact that she was
now willing to marry Arthur, without analyzing the
causes that had brought her to this decision, should
have warned her that she was dimly afraid of the
stranger. Her glance fell upon the mandarin's
ring. She twirled it round undecidedly. Should

she wear it or put it away? The question remained suspended. She saw Craig coming aboard; and she hid her face behind her magazine. Upon second thought she let the magazine fall. She was quite confident that that chapter was closed. Craig might be a scoundrel, but he was no fool.

A sharp blast from the tender's whistle drew her attention to the gangplank. The last man to come aboard was Warrington. He appeared in no especial hurry. He immediately sought James; and they stood together chatting until the tender drew up alongside the steamer of the British-India line. The two men shook hands finally. There seemed to be some argument, in which Warrington bore down the servant. The latter added a friendly tap on the Eurasian's shoulder. No one would have suspected that the white man and his dark companion had been "shipmates," in good times and in bad, for nearly a decade. Elsa, watching them from her secure nook, admired the lack of effusiveness. The dignity of the parting told her of the depth of feeling.

An hour later they were heading for the delta.

Elsa amused herself by casting bits of bread to

the gulls. Always they caught it on the wing, no matter in what direction she threw it. Sometimes one would wing up to her very hand for charity, its coral feet stretched out to meet the quick back-play of the wings, its cry shallow and plaintive and world-lonely.

Suddenly she became aware of a presence at her side.

A voice said: " It was not quite fair of you."

" What wasn't? " without turning her head. She brushed her hands free of the crumbs.

" You should have let me know that you were going to sail on this boat."

" You would have run away, then."

" Why? " startled at her insight.

" Because you are a little afraid of me." She faced him, without a smile either on her lips or in her eyes. " Aren't you? "

" Yes. I am afraid of all things I do not quite understand."

" There is not the least need in the world, Mr. Warrington. I am quite harmless. My claws have been clipped. I am engaged to be married, and am going home to decide the day."

CONFIDENCES

" He's a lucky man." He was astonished at his calm, for the blow went deep.

" Lucky? That is in the future. What a lonely thing a gull is ! "

" What a lonely thing a lonely man is ! " he added. Poor fool! To have dreamed so fair a dream for a single moment! He tried to believe that he was glad that she had told him about the other man. The least this information could do would be to give him better control of himself. He had not been out in the open long enough entirely to master his feelings.

" Men ought not to be lonely," she said. " There's the excitement of work, of mingling with crowds, of going when and where one pleases. A woman is hemmed in by a thousand petty must-nots. She can't go out after dark; she can't play whist or billiards, or sit at a table in the open and drink and smoke and spin yarns. Woman's lot is wondering and waiting at home. When I marry I suppose that I shall learn the truth of that."

Perhaps it was because he had been away from them so long and had lost track of the moods of the feminine mind; but surely it could not be possible that there was real happiness in this young woman's heart. Its evidence was lacking in her voice, in her face, in her gestures. He thought it over with a sigh. It was probably one of those marriages of convenience, money on one side and social position on the other. He felt sorry for the girl, sorry for the man; for it was not possible that a girl like this one would go through life without experiencing that flash of insanity that is called the grand passion.

He loved her. He could lean against the rail, his shoulder lightly touching hers, and calmly say to himself that he loved her. He could calmly permit her to pass out of his life as a cloud passes down the sea-rim. He hadn't enough, but this evil must befall him. Love! He spread out his hands unconsciously.

" What does that mean? " she asked, smiling now. " An invocation? "

" It's a sign to ward off evil," he returned.

" From whom? "

" From me."

" Are you expecting evil? "

" I am always preparing myself to meet it. There is one thing that will always puzzle me.

Why should you have asked the purser to pick out such a tramp as I was? For I was a tramp."

" I thought I explained that."

" Not clearly."

" Well, then, I shall make myself clear. The sight of you upon that bank, the lights in your face, struck me as the strangest mystery that could possibly confront me. I thought you were a ghost."

" A ghost? "

" Yes. So I asked the purser to introduce you to prove to my satisfaction that you weren't a ghost. Line for line, height for height, color for color, you are the exact counterpart of the man I am going home to marry."

She saw the shiver that ran over him; she saw his eyes widen; she saw his hands knot in pressure over the rail.

" The man you are going to marry! " he whispered.

Abruptly, without explanation, he walked away, his shoulders settled, his head bent. It was her turn to be amazed. What could this attitude mean?

" Mr. Warrington! " she called.

But he disappeared down the companionway.

VIII

A WOMAN'S REASON

ELSA stared at the vacant doorway. She recognized only a sense of bewilderment. This was not one of those childish flashes of rudeness that had amused, annoyed and mystified her. She had hurt him. And how? Her first explanation was instantly rejected as absurd, impossible. They had known each other less than a fortnight. They had exchanged opinions upon a thousand topics, but sentiment had had no visible part in these encounters. They had been together three days on the boat, and once he had taken tea with her in Rangoon. She could find nothing save that she had been kind to him when he most needed kindness, and that she had not been stupidly curious, only sympathetically so. He interested her and held that interest because he was a type unlike anything she had met outside the covers of a book. He was so big and strong, and yet so boyish. He had given her visions of the character which had carried his manhood through all these years of strife and bitterness and temptation. And because of this she had shown him that she had taken it for granted that whatever he had done in the past had not put him beyond the pale of her friendship. There had been no degrading entanglements, and women forgive or condone all other transgressions.

And what had she just said or done to put that look of dumb agony in his face? She swung impatiently from the rail. She hated abstruse problems, and not the least of these was that which would confront her when she returned to America. She began to promenade the deck, still cluttered with luggage over which the Lascar stewards were moiling. Many a glance followed the supple pleasing figure of the girl as she passed round and round the deck. Other promenaders stepped aside or permitted her to pass between. The resolute uplift of the chin, and the staring dark eyes which saw but inner visions, impressed them with the fact that it would be wiser to step aside voluntarily. There were some, however, who considered that they had as much right to the deck as she. Before them she would stop shortly, and as a current breaks and passes each side of an immovable object, they, too, gave way.

The colonel fussed and fumed, and his three spinster charges drew their pale lips into thinner paler lines.

" These Americans are impossible! "

" And it is scandalous the way the young women travel alone. One can never tell what they are."

" Humph! Brag and assertiveness. And there's that ruffian who came down the river. What's he doing on the same boat? What? "

Elsa became aware of their presence at the fifth turn. She nodded absently. Being immersed in the sea of conjecture regarding Warrington's behavior, the colonel's glare did not rouse in her the sense of impending disaster.

The first gong for dinner boomed. Elsa missed the clarion notes of the bugle, so familiar to her ears on the Atlantic. The echoing wail of the gong spoke in the voice of the East, of its dalliance, its content to drift in a sargassa sea of entangling habits and desires, of its fatalism and inertia. It did not hearten one or excite hunger. Elsa would

rather have lain down in her Canton lounging-chair.
The gong seemed out of place on the sea. Vaguely
it reminded her of the railway stations at home,
where they beat the gong to entice passengers into
the evil-smelling restaurants, there to lose their patience and often their trains.

The dining-saloon held two long tables, only one
of which was in commission, the starboard. The
saloon was unattractive, for staterooms marshaled
along each side of it; and one caught glimpses of
tumbled luggage and tousled berths. A punka
stretched from one end of the table to the other, and
swung indolently to and fro, whining mysteriously
as if in protest, sometimes subsiding altogether (as
the wearied coolie above the lights fell asleep) and
then flapping hysterically (after a shout of warning
from the captain) and setting the women's hair
awry.

Elsa and Martha were seated somewhere between
the head and the foot of the table. The personally-
conducted surrounded them, and gabbled incessantly
during the meal of what they had seen, of what they
were going to see, and of what they had missed by
not going with the other agency's party. Elsa's

sympathy went out to the tired and faded conductor.

There was but one vacant chair; and as she saw Warrington nowhere, Elsa assumed that this must be his reservation. She was rather glad that he would be beyond conversational radius. She liked to talk to the strange and lonely man, but she preferred to be alone with him when she did so. Neither of them had yet descended to the level of trifles; and Elsa had no wish to share with persons uninteresting and uncompanionable her serious views of life. Sometimes she wondered if, after all, she was not as old as the hills instead of twenty-five.

She began as of old to study carelessly the faces of the diners and to speculate as to their characters and occupations. Her negligent observation roved from the pompous captain down to the dark picturesque face of the man Craig. Upon him her glance, a mixture of contempt and curiosity, rested. If he behaved himself and made no attempt to speak to her, she was willing to declare a truce. In Rangoon the man had been drunk, but on the Irrawaddy boat he had been sober enough. Craig kept his eyes directed upon his food and did not offer her even a furtive glance.

He was not in a happy state of mind. He had taken passage the last moment to avoid meeting again the one man he feared. For ten years this man had been reckoned among the lost. Many believed him dead, and Craig had wished it rather than believed. And then, to meet him face to face in that sordid boarding-house had shaken the cool nerve of the gambler. He was worried and bewildered. He had practically sent this man to ruin. What would be the reprisal? He reached for a mangosteen and ate the white pulpy contents, but without the customary relish. The phrase kept running through his head: What would be the reprisal? For men of his ilk never struck without expecting to be struck back. Something must be done. Should he seek him and boldly ask what he intended to do? Certainly he could not do much on board here, except to denounce him to the officers as a professional gambler. And Paul would scarcely do that since he, Craig, had a better shot in his gun. He could tell who Paul was and what he had done. Bodily harm was what he really feared.

He had seen Elsa, but he had worked out that problem easily.   She was sure to say nothing so long as he let her be; and with the episode of the hat-pin still fresh in his memory, he assuredly would keep his distance.   He had made a mistake, and was not likely to repeat it.

But Paul! He finished his dessert and went off to the stuffy little smoke-room, and struggled with a Burma cheroot.   Paul was a smoker, and sooner or later he would drop in.   There would be no beating about the bush on his part.   If it was to be war, all right; a truce, well and good.   But he wanted to know, and he was not going to let fear stand in the way.   He waited in vain for his man that night.

And so did Elsa.   She felt indignant at one moment and hurt at another.   The man's attitude was inexplicable; there was neither rhyme nor reason in it.   The very fact that she could not understand made her wonder march beside her even in her dreams that night.   She began to feel genuinely sorry that he had appeared above her horizon.   He had disturbed her poise; he had thrown her accepted views of life into an entirely different angle, kaleido-scopically.   And always that supernatural likeness to the other man. Elsa began to experience a sensation like that which attends the imagination of one in the clutch of a nightmare: she hung in mid-air: she could neither retreat nor go forward. Just before she retired she leaned over the rail, watching the reflection of the stars twist and shiver on the smooth water. Suddenly she listened. She might have imagined it, for at night the ears deceive. " Jah, jah!" Somewhere from below came the muffled plaint of Rajah.

Next day, at luncheon, the chair was still vacant. Elsa became alarmed. Perhaps he was ill. She made inquiries, regardless of the possible misinterpretation her concern might be given by others. Mr. Warrington had had his meals served in his cabin, but the steward declared that the gentleman was not ill, only tired and irritable, and that he amused himself with a trained parrakeet.

All day long the sea lay waveless and unrippled, a sea of brass and lapis-lazuli; brass where the sun struck and lapis-lazuli in the shadow of the lazy swells. Schools of flying-fish broke fan-wise in flashes of silver, and porpoise sported alongside. And warmer and warmer grew the air.

Starboard was rigged up for cricket, and the ship's officers and some of the passengers played the game until the first gong. Elsa grumbled to Martha. There was little enough space to walk in as it was without the men taking over the whole side of the ship and cheating her out of a glorious sunset. Martha grew troubled and perplexed. If there was one phase of character unknown to her in Elsa it was irritability; and here she was, finding fault like any ordinary tourist.

"Where is Mr. Warrington?"

"I don't know. I haven't seen him since yesterday." Elsa dropped her book petulantly. "I am weary of these namby-pamby stories."

"Why, I thought you admired that author."

"Not to-day at any rate. Silly twaddle."

Martha's eyes had a hopeless look in them as she asked: "Elsa, what is the matter?"

"I don't know, Martha. I believe I should like to lose my temper utterly. It might be a great relief."

"It's the climate."

"It may be. But it's my belief I'm irritable because I do not know my own mind. I hate the stuffy stateroom, the food, the captain."

" The captain? "

" Yes. Nothing seems to disturb his conceit. To-night we sleep on deck, the starboard side. At five o'clock we have to get up and go inside again so they can holystone the deck. And I am always soundest asleep at that time. Doubtless, I shall be irritable all day to-morrow."

" Sleep up here on deck? " horrified.

" That, or suffocate below."

" But the men? "

" They sleep on the port side." Elsa laughed maliciously. " Don't worry. Nobody minds."

" I hate the East," declared Martha vindictively. " Everything is so slack. It just brings out the shiftlessness in everybody."

" Perhaps that is what ails me; I am growing shiftless. When I came on board I decided to marry Arthur, and have done with the pother. Now I am at the same place as when I left home. I don t want to marry anybody. Have you noticed that fellow Craig? "

"What will you do if he speaks?"

"I have half a dozen good hat-pins left," dryly.

"I hate to hear you talk like that."

"It's the East. . . . There goes that hateful gong again. Soup, chicken, curry, rice and piccalilli. I am going to live on plantains and mangosteens. I'm glad we had sense enough to order that distilled water. I should die if I had to drink any more soda. I wish I had booked straight through. I shall be bored to death in Japan, much as I wish to see the cherry-blossom dance. Probably I shan't enjoy anything. Come; we'll go down as we are to dinner, and watch the ridiculous captain and his fan-bearer. The punka will at least give us a breath of fresh air. There doesn't seem to be any on deck. One regrets Darjeeling."

Martha followed her young mistress into the dining-saloon; she was anxious and upset. Where would this mood end? With a glance of relief she found Warrington's chair still vacant.

The saloon had an air of freshness to-night. All the men were in drill or pongee, and so receptive is the imagination that the picture robbed the room of half its heat. To and fro the punka flapped; the pulleys creaked and the ropes scraped above the sound of knives and forks and spoons.

Elsa ate little besides fruit. She spoke scarcely a word to Martha, and none to those around her. Thus, she missed the frown of the colonel and the lifted brows of the spinsters, and the curious glances of the tourists. The passenger-list had not yet come from the ship's press, so Elsa's name was practically unknown. But in some unaccountable manner it had become known that she had been making inquiries in regard to the gentleman in cabin 78, who had thus far remained away from the table. Ship life is a dull life, and gossip is about the only thing that makes it possible to live through the day. It was quite easy to couple this unknown aloof young woman and the invisible man, and then to wait for results. The average tourist is invariably building a romance around those persons who interest them, attractively or repellently. They have usually saturated their minds with impossible impressions of the East, acquired long before they visit it, and refuse to accept actualities. It would have amused Elsa had she known the interest she had already created if not inspired. Her beauty and her apparent indifference to her surroundings were particularly adapted to the romantic mood of her fellow-travelers. Her own mind was so broad and generous, so high and detached, that so sordid a thing as " an affair " never entered her thoughts.

As she refused course after course, a single phrase drummed incessantly through her tired brain. She was not going to marry Arthur; never, never in this world. She did not love him, and this was to be final. She would cable him from Singapore. But she felt no elation in having arrived at this determination. In fact, there was a tingle of defiance in her unwritten, unspoken ultimatum.

That night Craig found it insupportable in the cabin below; so he ordered his steward to bring up his bedding. He had lain down for half an hour, grown restless, and had begun to walk the deck in his bath-slippers. He had noted the still white figure forward, where the cross-rail marks the waist. As he approached, Craig discovered his man. He hesitated only a moment; then he touched Warrington's arm.

Warrington turned his dull eyes upon his ancient

enemy. "So it is you? I understood you were on board. Well?" uncompromisingly.

"I've been looking for you. Bygones are bygones, and what's done can't be undone by punching a fellow's head. I'm not looking for trouble," went on Craig, gaining assurance. "I am practically down and out myself. I can't go back to the States for a while. All I want is to get to Hongkong in peace for the April races. What stand are you going to take on board here? That's all I want to know."

"It would give me great pleasure, Craig, to take you by the scruff of your neck and drop you overboard. But as you say, what's been done can't be remedied by bashing in a man's head. Well, here you are, since you ask. If you speak to me, if I catch you playing cards or auctioneering a pool, if you make yourself obnoxious to any of the passengers, I promise to give you the finest thrashing you ever had, the moment we reach Penang. If you don't go ashore there, I'll do it in Singapore. Have I made myself clear?"

"That's square enough, Paul," said the gambler resignedly. There wasn't much money on board these two-by-four boats, anyhow, so he wasn't losing much.

Warrington leaned forward. " Paul? You said Paul?"

" Why, yes," wonderingly.

" Better go."

" All right." Craig returned to his mattress. " Now, what made him curl up like that because I called him Paul? Bah!" He dug a hole in his pillow and tried to sleep.

" Paul!" murmured Warrington.

He stared down at the flashes of phosphorescence, blindly. The man had called him Paul. After ten years to learn the damnable treachery of it! Suddenly he clenched his hand and struck the rail. He would go back. All his loyalty, all his chivalry, had gone for naught. This low rascal had called him Paul.

IX

W HEN Elsa stepped out of the companionway the next morning she winced and shut
her eyes. The whole arc of heaven seemed hung
with fire-opals; east, west, north and south, which-
ever way she looked, there was dazzling iridescence.
The long flowing swells ran into the very sky, for
there was visible no horizon. Gold-leaf and opals,
thought Elsa. What a wonderful world! What a
versatile mistress was nature! Never two days
alike, never two human beings; animate and inani-
mate, all things were singular. She paused at the
rail and glanced down the rusty black side of the
ship and watched the thread of frothing water that
clutched futilely at the red water-line. Never two
living things alike, in all the millions and millions
swarming the globe. What a marvel! Even
though this man Warrington and Arthur looked

alike, they were not so. In heart and mind they were as different as two days.

She began her usual walk, and in passing the smoke-room door on the port side she met Warrington coming out. How deep-set his eyes were! He was about to go on, but she looked straight into his eyes, and he stopped. She laughed, and held out her hand.

" I really believe you were going to snub me."

" Then you haven't given me up? "

" Never mind what I have or have not done. Walk with me. I am going to talk plainly to you. If what I say is distasteful, don't hesitate to interrupt me. You interest me, partly because you act like a boy, partly because you are a man."

" I haven't any manners."

" They need shaking up and readjusting. I have just been musing over a remarkable thing, that no two objects are alike. Even the most accurate machinery can not produce two nails without variation. So it is with humans. You look so like the man I know back home that it is impossible not to ponder over you." She smiled into his face. " Why should nature produce two persons who are mis-

taken for each other, and yet give them two souls,
two intellects, totally different?"

"I have often wondered."

"Is nature experimenting, or is she slyly playing
a trick on humanity?"

"Let us call it a trick; by all means, let us call
it that."

"Your tone . . ."

"Yes, yes," impatiently; "you are going to say
that it sounds bitter. But why should another man
have a face like mine, when we have nothing in
common? What right has he to look like me?"

"It is a puzzle," Elsa admitted.

"This man who looks like me — I have no doubt
it affects you oddly — probably lives in ease; never
knew what a buffet meant, never knew what a care
was, has everything he wants; in fact, a gentleman
of your own class, whose likes and dislikes are cut
from the same pattern as your own. Well, that is
as it should be. A woman such as you are ought
to marry an equal, a man whose mind and manners
are fitted to the high place he holds in your affection
and in your world. How many worlds there are,
man-made and heaven-made, and each as deadly as

the other, as cold and implacable! To you, who
have been kind to me, I have acted like a fool. The
truth is, I've been skulking. My vanity was hurt.
I had the idea that it was myself and not my resemblance that appealed to your interest. What
makes you trust me?" bluntly; and he stopped as he
asked the question.

"Why, I don't know," blankly. Instantly she
recovered herself. "But I do trust you." She
walked on, and perforce he fell into her stride.

"It is because you trust the other man."

"Thanks. That is it precisely; and for nearly
two weeks I've been trying to solve that very thing."

After a pause he asked: "Have you ever read
Reade's *Singleheart and Doubleface?*"

"Yes. But what bearing has it upon our discussion?"

"None that you would understand," evasively.
His tongue had nearly tripped him.

"Are you sure?"

"Of this, that I shall never understand women."

"Do not try to," she advised. "All those men
who knew most about women were the unhappiest."

They made a round in silence. Passengers were

beginning to get into their deck-chairs; and Elsa noted the backs of the many novels that ranged from the pure chill altitudes of classic and demi-classics down to the latest popular yarn. Many an eye peered over the tops of the books; and envy and admiration and curiosity brought their shafts to bear upon her. It was something to create these variant expressions of interest. She was oblivious.

"We stop at Penang?" she asked.

"Five or six hours, long enough to see the town."

"We went directly from Singapore to Colombo, so we missed the town coming out. I should like to see that cocoanut plantation of yours."

"It is too far inland. Besides, I am *a persona non grata* there." As, indeed, he was. His heart burned with shame and rage at the recollection of the last day there. Three or four times, during the decade, the misfortune of being found out had fallen to his lot, and always when he was employed at something worth while.

Elsa discreetly veered into another channel. "You will go back to Italy, I suppose. How cheaply and delightfully one may live there, when one knows something of the people! I had the Villa

Julia one spring. You know it; Sorrento. Is there anything more stunning than oranges in the rain?" irrelevantly.

"Yes, I shall go to Italy once more. But first I am going home." He was not aware of the grimness that entered his voice as he made this statement.

"I am glad," she said. "After all, that is the one place."

"If you are happy enough to find a welcome."

"And you will see your mother again?"

He winced. "Yes. Do you know, it does not seem possible that I met you but two short weeks ago? I have never given much thought to this so-called reincarnation; but somewhere in the past ages I knew you; only . . ."

"Only what?"

"Only, you weren't going home to marry the other fellow."

She stopped at the rail. "Who knows?" she replied ruminatingly. "Perhaps I am not going to marry him."

"Don't you love him? . . . I beg your pardon, Miss Chetwood!"

TWO SHORT WEEKS

" You're excused."

" I still need some training. I have been alone so much that I haven't got over the trick of speaking my thoughts aloud."

" No harm has been done. The fault lay with me."

" I used to learn whole pages from stories and recite them to the trees or to the parrot. It kept me from going mad, I believe. In camp I handled coolies; none of whom could speak a word of English. I didn't have James with me at that time. During the day I was busy enough seeing that they did their work well. When things ran smoothly I'd take out a book and study. At night I'd stand before my tent and declaim. I could not read at night. If I lighted a lantern the tent would become alive with abominable insects. So I'd declaim, merely to hear the sound of my voice. Afterward I learned that the coolies looked upon me as a holy man. They believed I was nightly offering prayers to one of my gods. Perhaps I was; the god of reason. In the mornings I used to have to shake my boots. Frogs and snakes would get in during the night, the latter in search of the former.

Lively times! All that seems like a bad dream now."

"And how is Rajah?"

"Ugly as ever."

"Are you going to take him with you?"

"Wherever I go. Looks silly, doesn't it, for a man of my size to tote around a parrot-cage? But I don't care what people think. Life is too short. It's what you think of yourself that really counts."

"That is one of the rules I have laid down for myself. If only we all might go through life with that idea! There wouldn't be any gossip or scandal, then."

"Some day I am going to tell you why I have lived over here all these years."

"I shouldn't, not if it hurts you."

"On the contrary, there's a kind of happiness in unburdening one's conscience. I called that day in Rangoon for the express purpose of telling you everything, but I couldn't in the presence of a third person."

"I do not demand it."

"But it's a duty I owe to myself," he insisted

gravely. " Besides, it is not impossible that you may hear the tale from other lips; and I rather prefer to tell it myself."

" But always remember that I haven't asked you."

" Are you afraid to hear it? "

" No. What I am trying to convince you with is the fact that I trust you, and that I give you my friendship without reservations."

He laid his hand on hers, strongly. " God bless you for that! "

She liked him because there was lacking in his words and tones that element of flattery so distasteful to her. Men generally entertain the fallacy that a woman demands homage, first to her physical appearance, next to her taste in gowns, and finally to her intellect, when in the majority of cases it is the other way around. Elsa knew that she was beautiful, but it no longer interested her to hear men state the fact, knowing as she did that it was simply to win her good will.

" Would you like to sit next to me at the table? "

" May I? " eagerly.

" I'll have Martha change her chair for yours. Do you speak Italian? "

"Enough for ordinary conversation. It is a long time since I have spoken the tongue."

"Then, let us talk it as much as possible at the table, if only to annoy those around us."

He laughed.

"I was educated in Rome," she added.

"Are you religious?"

Elsa shrugged. "At present I don't know just what my religion is. Scandalous, isn't it? But for many weeks a thousand gods have beset me. I've got to get back to civilization in order to readjust my views. At luncheon, then. I am beginning to feel snoozy."

Craig had been eying the two, evilly. Set the wind in that direction? An idea found soil in his mind, and grew. He would put a kink, as he vulgarly expressed it, into that affair. He himself wasn't good enough for her. The little cat should see. Warrington's ultimatum of the night before burned and rankled, and a man of Craig's caliber never accepted the inevitable without meditating revenge, revenge of a roundabout character, such as would insure his physical safety. The man could not play fair; there was nothing either in his heart or in his mind upon which square play could find foothold. There was nothing loyal or generous or worthy in the man. There is something admirable in a great rascal; but a sordid one is a pitiful thing. Craig entered the smoke-room and ordered a peg. At luncheon he saw them sitting together, and he smothered a grin. Couldn't play cards, or engineer a pool, eh? All right. There were other amusements.

That afternoon Martha chanced to sit down in a vacant chair, just out of the range of the cricketers. She lolled back and idly watched the batsmen. And then she heard voices.

"She is Elsa Chetwood. I remember seeing her pictures. She is a society girl, very wealthy, but something of a snob."

Martha's ears tingled. A snob, indeed, because she minded principally her own affairs!

"They think because they belong to the exclusive sets they can break as many laws of convention as they please. Well, they can't. There's always some scandal in the papers about them. There was some rumor of her being engaged to the Duke of What's-his-name, but it fell through because she wouldn't settle a fortune on him. Only sensible thing she ever did, probably."

"And did you notice who sat next to her at luncheon?"

"A gentleman with a past, Mr. Craig tells me."

"I dare say Miss Chetwood has a past, too, if one but knew. To travel alone like this!"

Busybodies! Martha rose indignantly and returned to the other side of the deck. Meddlers! What did they know? To peck like daws at one so far above them, so divinely far above them! Her natural impulse had been to turn upon them and give them the tongue-lashing they deserved. But she had lived too long with Elsa not to have learned self-repression, and that the victory is always with those who stoop not to answer. Nevertheless, she was alarmed. Elsa must be warned.

All Elsa said was: "My dear Martha, in a few days they and their tittle-tattle will pass out of my existence, admitting that they have ever entered it. I repeat, my life is all my own, and that I am concerned only with those whom I wish to retain as my friends. Gossip is the shibboleth of the mediocre, and, thank heaven, I am not mediocre."

TWO SHORT WEEKS

While dressing for dinner Elsa discovered a note on the floor of her cabin. The writing was unfamiliar. She opened it and sought first the signature. Slowly her cheeks reddened, and her lips twisted in disdain. She did not read the note, but the natural keenness of her eye caught the name of Warrington. She tore the letter into scraps which she tossed out the port-hole. What a vile thing the man was! He had had the effrontery to sign his name. He must be punished.

It was as late as ten o'clock when she and Warrington went up to the bow and gazed down the cutwater. Never had she seen anything so weirdly beautiful as the ribbons of phosphorescence which fell away on each side, luminously blue and flaked with dancing starlike particles, through which, ever and anon, flying-fish, dripping with the fire, spun outward like tongues of flame.

" Beautiful, beautiful! This is the one spot on the ship. And in all my travels I have never seen this before. All silence and darkness in front of us, and beneath, that wonderful fire. Thanks for bringing me here. I should not have known what I was missing."

"Often, when I was stoking, during an hour or so of relief, I used to steal up here and look down at the mystery, for it will ever be a mystery to me. And I found comfort."

"Are you religious, too?"

"In one thing, that God demands that every man shall have faith in himself."

How deep his voice was as compared to Arthur's! Arthur. Elsa frowned at the rippling magic. Why was she invariably comparing the two men? What significance did it have upon the future, since, at the present moment, it was not understandable?

"There is a man on board by the name of Craig," she said. "I advise you to beware of him."

"Who introduced him to you?" The anger in his voice was very agreeable to her ears. "Who dared to?"

"No one. He introduced himself on the way up to Mandalay. In Rangoon I closed the acquaintance, such as it was, with the aid of a hat-pin."

"A hat-pin! What did he say to you?" roughly.

"Nothing that I care to repeat. . . . Stop! I am perfectly able to take care of myself. I do not need any valiant champion."

TWO SHORT WEEKS

"He has spoken to you about me?"

"A letter. I saw only his name and yours. I tore it up and threw it overboard. Let us go back. Somehow, everything seems spoiled. I am sorry I spoke."

"I shall see that he does not bother you again," ominously.

They returned to the promenade deck in silence.

When Warrington found Craig the man was helplessly intoxicated. He lay sprawled upon his mattress, and the kick administered did not stir him. Warrington looked down at the sodden wretch moodily.

Craig's intoxication was fortunate for him, otherwise he would have been roughly handled; for there was black murder in the heart of the broken man standing above him. Warrington relaxed his clenched hands. This evil-breathing thing at his feet was the primal cause of it all, he and a man's damnable weakness. Of what use his new-found fortune? Better for him had he stayed in the jungle, better have died there, hugging his poor delusion. Oh, abysmal fool that he had been!

X

THE CUT DIRECT

IT was after five in the morning when the deck-
hands tried to get Craig to go down to his room.
With the dull obstinacy of a drunken man, he refused to stir; he was perfectly satisfied to stay where
he was. The three brown men stood irresolutely
and helplessly around the man. Every one had gone
below. The hose was ready to flush the deck. It
did not matter; he, Craig, would not budge.

"Leave me alone, you black beggars!"

"But, Sahib," began one of the Lascars, who
spoke English.

"Don't talk to me. I tell you, get out!" strik-
ing at their feet with his swollen hands.

Warrington, who had not lain down at all, but
who had wandered about the free decks like some
lost soul from *The Flying Dutchman*, Warrington,
hearing voices, came out of the smoke-room. A

glance was sufficient. A devil's humor took possession of him. He walked over.

"Get up," he said quietly.

Craig blinked up at him from out of puffed eyes. "Go to the devil! Fine specimen to order *me* about."

"Will you get up peacefully? These men have work to do."

Craig was blind to his danger. "What's that to me? 'Go away, all of you, to the devil, for all I care. I'll get up when I get damn good and ready. Not before."

Warrington picked up the hose.

"Sahib!" cried the Lascar in protest.

"Be still!" ordered Warrington. "Craig, for the last time, will you get up?"

"No!"

Warrington turned the key, and a deluge of cold salt-water struck Craig full in the chest. He tried to sit up, but was knocked flat. Then he rolled over on the deck, choking and sputtering. He crawled on his hands and knees until he reached the chair-rail, which he clutched desperately, drawing himself up. The pitiless stream never swerved. It smacked against the flat of his back like the impact of a hand.

"For God's sake stop it!" cried Craig, half strangled.

"Will you go below?"

"Yes, yes! Turn it away!" sober enough by now.

Warrington switched off the key, his face humorless, though there was a sparkle of grim humor in his sleep-hungry eyes. Craig leaned against the deck-house, shaking and panting.

"I would I could get at your soul as easily." Warrington threw aside the hose, and the Lascars sprang upon it, not knowing what the big blond Sahib might do next.

Craig turned, venom on his tongue. He spoke a phrase. In an instant, cold with fury, Warrington had him by the throat.

"You low base cur!" he said, shaking the man until he resembled a manikin on wires. "Had you been sober last night, I'd have thrown you into the sea. Honorless dog! You wrote to Miss Chetwood. You insulted her, too. If you wish to die, speak to her again."

THE CUT DIRECT

Craig struggled fiercely to free himself. He wasn't sure, by the look of the other man's eyes, that he wasn't going to be killed then and there. There was something cave-mannish and cruel in the way Warrington worried the man, shaking him from side to side and forcing him along the deck. Suddenly he released his hold, adding a buffet on the side of the head that sent Craig reeling and sobbing into the companionway.

"Here, I say, what's the row?"

Warrington looked over his shoulder. The call had come from the first officer.

"A case of drunkenness," coolly.

"But I say, we can't have brawling on deck, sir. You ought to know that. If the man's conduct was out of order, you should have brought your complaint before the captain or me. We really can't have any rowing, sir."

Warrington replied gravely: "Expediency was quite necessary."

"What's this?" The officer espied the soaked bedding. "Who turned the hose here?"

"I did," answered Warrington.

"I shall have to report that to the captain, sir.

139

It's against the rules aboard this steamship for passengers to touch anything of that sort." The officer turned and began violently to abuse the bewildered Lascars.

" I shouldn't bullyrag them, sir," interposed Warrington. " They protested. I helped myself. After all, perhaps it was none of my affair; but the poor devils didn't know what to do."

The officer ordered the Lascars to take the mattress and throw it on the boat-deck, where it would dry quickly when the sun rose. Already the world was pale with light, and a slash of crimson lay low on the rim of the east.

" I shouldn't like to be disagreeable, sir," said the officer. " I dare say the man made himself obnoxious; but I'm obliged to report anything of this order."

" Don't be alarmed on my account. My name is Warrington, cabin 78. Good morning."

Warrington entered the companionway; and a moment later he heard the water hiss along the deck. He was not in the least sorry for what he had done; still, he regretted the act. Craig was a beast, and there was no knowing what he might do or say.

But the hose had been simply irresistible. He chuckled audibly on the way down to his cabin. There was one thing of which he was assured; Craig would keep out of his way in the future. The exhilaration of the struggle suddenly left him, and he realized that he was dreadfully tired and heart-achy. Still dressed, he flung himself in his bunk, and immediately fell into a heavy dreamless sleep that endured until luncheon.

Shortly after luncheon something happened down in the engine-room; and the chief engineer said that they would have to travel at half speed to Penang. In other words, they would not make the port to-day, Sunday, but to-morrow. Another day with this mysterious tantalizing woman, thought Warrington. He went in search of her, but before he found her, he was summoned to the captain's cabin. Warrington presented himself, mildly curious. The captain nodded to a stool.

" Sit down, Mr. Warrington. Will you have a cheroot? "

" Yes, thanks."

A crackle of matches followed.

" This fellow Craig has complained about his

treatment by you this morning. I fancy you were rather rough with him."

"Perhaps. He was very drunk and abusive, and he needed cold water more than anything else. I once knew the man."

"Ah! But it never pays to manhandle that particular brand of tippler. They always retaliate in some way."

"I suppose he has given you an excerpt from my history?"

"He says you can not return to the States."

"I am returning on the very first boats I can find."

"Then he was lying?"

"Not entirely. I do not know what he has told you, and I really do not care. The fact is, Craig is a professional gambler, and I warned him not to try any of his tricks on board. It soured him."

"And knowing myself that he was a professional, I gave no weight to his accusations. Besides, it is none of my business. The worst scoundrel unhung has certain rights on my ship. If he behaves himself, that is sufficient for me. Now, what Craig told me doesn't matter; but it matters that I warned him. A word to any one else, and I'll drop him at Penang to-morrow, to get out the best way he can. Ships passing there this time of year are generally full-up. Will you have a peg?"

"No, thanks. But I wish to say that it is very decent of you." Warrington rose.

"I have traveled too long not to recognize a man when I see him. Do you play cricket?" asked the captain, his gaze critically covering the man before him.

"No; I regret I'm not familiar with the game."

"Ah! well, drop in any night after ten, if you care to."

"I shall be glad to accept your hospitality."

Outside, Warrington mused on the general untruths of first impressions. He had written down the captain as a pompous, self-centered individual. One never could judge a man until he came to the scratch. It heartened him to find that there was a man on board who respected his misfortune, whether he believed it or not. He sought Elsa, and as they promenaded, lightly recounted the episode of the morning.

143

Elsa expressed her delight in laughter that was less hearty than malicious. How clearly she could see the picture! And then, the ever-recurring comparisons: Arthur would have gone by, Arthur would not have bothered himself, for he detested scenes and fisticuffs. How few real men she had met, men who walked through life naturally, unfettered by those self-applied manacles called "What will people say?"

"Let us go up to the bow," she invited. "I've a little story myself to tell."

They clambered down and up the ladders, over the windlass and anchor-chains which a native was busily painting. A school of porpoise were frolicking under the cutwater. *Plop! plop!* they went; and sometimes one would turn sidewise and look up roguishly with his twinkling seal-like eyes. *Plop! plop!* Finally all save one sank gracefully out of sight. The laggard crisscrossed the cutwater a dozen times, just to show the watchers how extremely clever he was; and then, with a *plop!* that was louder than any previous one, he vanished into the deeps.

"I love these Oriental seas," said Elsa, with her

arms on the rail and her chin resting upon them. She wore no hat, and her hair shimmered in the sun and shivered in the wind.

"And yet they are the most treacherous of all seas. There's not a cloud in sight; in two hours from now we may be in the heart of a winter storm. Happily, they are rarities along this coast; so you will not have the excitement of a ship-wreck."

"I am grateful for that. Mercy! Think of being marooned on a desert island with the colonel and his three spinsters! Proprieties, from morning until night. And the chattering tourists! Heaven forfend!"

"You had a story to tell me," he suggested. His heart was hot within him. He wanted to sweep her up in his arms and hold her there forever. But the barrier of wasted opportunities stood between. How delicately beautiful she was: Bernini's Daphne.

"Oh, yes; I had almost forgotten." She stood up and felt for wandering strands of hair. "I find the world more amusing day by day. I ought to feel hurt, but I am only amused. I spoke to the colonel this morning, merely to say howdy-do. He stared me in the eye and de-lib-erately turned his back to me."

" The doddering old —"

" There, there! It isn't worth getting angry about."

" But, don't you understand? It's all because of me. Simply because you have been kind to a poor devil, they start in to snub you, you! I'll go back to my old seat at the table. You mustn't walk with me any more."

" Don't be silly. If you return to your chair, if you no longer walk with me, they'll find a thousand things to talk about. Since I do not care, why should you?"

" Can't I make it clear to you?" desperately.

" I see with reasonable eyes, if that is what you mean. The people I know, mine own people, understand Elsa Chetwood."

So her name was Elsa? He repeated it over and over in his mind.

She continued her exposition. " There are but few, gently born. They are generous and broad-minded. They could not be mine own people other-

wise. They are all I care about. I shun mediocrity as I would the plague. I refuse to permit it
to touch me, either with words or with deeds. The
good opinion of those I love is dear to me; as for
the rest of the world!" She snapped her fingers to
illustrate how little she cared.

"I am a man under a cloud, to be avoided."

"Perhaps that cloud has a silver lining," with a
gentle smile. "I do not believe you did anything
wrong, premeditatively. All of us, one time or another, surrender to wild impulse. Perhaps in the
future there awaits for me such a moment. I can-
not recollect the name of Warrington in a *cause
célèbre*," thoughtfully.

He could only gaze at her dumbly.

"Don't you suppose there is a vast difference
between you and this man Craig? Could you com-
mit the petty crime of cheating at cards, of taking
advantage of a woman's kindness, of betraying a
man's misfortune? I do not think you could. No,
Mr. Warrington, I do not care what they say, on
board here or elsewhere."

"My name is not Warrington," finding his voice.

God in heaven, what would happen when she found out what his name was? "But my first name is Paul."

"Paul. I have had my suspicions that your name was not Warrington. But tell me nothing more. What good would it do? I did not read that man's letter. I merely noted your name and his. You doubtless knew him somewhere in the past."

"Might there not be danger in your kindness to me?"

"In what way?"

"A man under a cloud is often reckless and desperate. There is always an invisible demon calling out to him: What's the use of being good? You are the first woman of your station who has treated me as a human being; I do not say as an equal. You have given me back some of my self-respect. It throws my world upside down. It's a heady wine for an abstemious man. Don't you realize that you are a beautiful woman?"

She looked up into his eyes quickly, but she saw nothing there indicating flattery, only a somber gravity.

"I should be silly to deny it. I know that had I

148

been a frump, the colonel would not have snubbed me. I wonder why it is that in life beauty in a woman is always looked upon with suspicion?"

"Envy provokes that."

She resumed her inclination against the rail again. "After Singapore it is probable that we shall not meet again. I admit, in my world, I could not walk upon this free and easy ground. I should have to ask about your antecedents, what you have done, all about you, in fact. Then, we should sit in judgment."

"And condemn me, off-hand. That would be perfectly right."

"But I might be one of the dissenting judges."

"That is because you are one woman in a thousand."

"No; I simply have a mind of my own, and often prefer to be guided by it. I am not a sheep."

Silence. The lap-lap of the water, the long slow rise and fall, and the dartling flying-fish apparently claimed their attention.

But Warrington saw nothing save the danger, the danger to himself and to her. At any moment he might fling his arms around her, without his having the power to resist. She called to him as nothing in the world had called before. But she trusted him, and because of this he resolutely throttled the recurring desires. She was right. He had scorned what she had termed as woman's instinct. She had read him with a degree of accuracy. In the eyes of God he was a good man, a dependable man; but he was not impossibly good. He was human enough to want her, human enough to appreciate the danger in which she stood of him. He was determined not to fail her. When she went back to her own world she would carry an unsullied memory of him. But, before God, *he* should not have her.

"Why did you do that?" she asked whimsically.

"Do what?"

"Shut your jaws with a snap."

"I was not conscious of the act."

"But you were thinking strongly about something."

"I was. Tell me about the man who looks like me." His gaze roved out to sea, to the white islands of vapor low-lying in the east. "In what respect does he resemble me?"

"His hair is yellow, his eyes are blue, and he smiles the same way you do."

He felt the lump rise and swell in his throat.

"If you stood before a mirror you would see him. But there the resemblance ends."

"You say that sadly. Why?"

"Did I? Well, perhaps I was thinking strongly, too."

"Is he a man who does things?" a note of strained curiosity in his tones. Ten years!

"In what way do you mean?"

"Does he work in the world, does he invent, build, finance?"

Mayhap her eyes deceived her, but the tan on his face seemed less brown than yellow.

"No; Mr. Ellison is a collector of paintings, of rugs, of rare old books and china. He's a bit detached, as dreamers usually are. He has written a book of exquisite verses. . . . You are smiling," she broke off suddenly, her eyes filling with cold lights.

"A thousand pardons! The thought was going through my head how unlike we are indeed. I can hardly tell one master from another, all old books look alike to me, and the same with china. I know something about rugs; but I couldn't write a jingle if it was to save me from hanging."

"Do you invent, build, finance?" A bit of a gulf had opened up between them. Elsa might not be prepared to marry Arthur, but she certainly would not tolerate a covert sneer in regard to his accomplishments.

Quietly and with dignity he answered: "I have built bridges in my time over which trains are passing at this moment. I have fought torrents, and floods, and hurricanes, and myself. I have done a man's work. I had a future, they said. But here I am, a subject of your pity."

She instantly relented. "But you are young. You can begin again."

"Not in the sense you mean."

"And yet, you tell me you are going back home,"

"Like a thief in the night," bitterly.

XI

THE BLUE FEATHER

ELSA toyed with her emeralds, apparently searching for some flaw. Like a thief in the night was a phrase that rang unpleasantly in her ears. Her remarkable interest in the man was neither to be denied nor ignored. In fact, drawing her first by the resemblance to the man she wanted to love but could not, and then by the mystery that he had thrown about his past simply by guarding it closely, it would have been far more remarkable if she had not been deeply interested in him. But to-night she paused for a moment. A little doubt, like one of those oblique flaws that obscured the clarity of the green stones, appeared. She had always been more or less indifferent to public opinion, but it had been a careless thoughtless indifference; it had not possessed the insolent twist of the past fortnight. To receive the cut direct from a man whose pomposity and mental density had excited her wit and amusement, surprised her even if it did not hurt. It had rudely awakened her to the fact that her independence might be leading her into a labyrinth. She was compelled to admit that at home she would have avoided Warrington, no matter how deeply sorry she might have been. His insistent warning against himself, however, served to arouse nothing more than a subtle obstinacy to do just as she pleased. And it pleased her to talk to him; it pleased her to trifle with the unknown danger.

Something new had been born in her. All her life she had gone about calmly and aloofly, her head in the clouds, her feet on mountain-tops. She had never done anything to arouse discussion in other women. Perhaps such a situation had never confronted her until lately. She had always looked forth upon life through the lenses of mild cynicism. So long as she was rich she might, with impunity, be as indiscreet as she pleased. Her money would plead forgiveness and toleration. . . . Elsa shrugged. But shrugs do not dismiss problems. She could have laughed. To have come all this way to solve a riddle, only to find a second more confusing than the first!

Like a thief in the night. She did not care to know what he had done, not half so much as to learn what he had been. Peculations of some order; of this she was reasonably sure. So why seek for details, when these might be sordid?

Singapore would see the end, and she would become her normal self again.

She clasped the necklace around her lovely throat. She was dressing for dinner, really dressing. An impish mood filled her with the irrepressible desire to shine in all her splendor to-night. Covertly she would watch the eyes of mediocrity widen. Hitherto they had seen her in the simple white of travel. To-night they should behold the woman who had been notable among the beauties in Paris, Vienna, Rome, London; who had not married a duke simply because his title could not have added to the security of her position, socially or financially; who was twenty-five years of age and perfectly content to wait until she met the man who would set to flight all the doubt which kept her heart unruly and unsettled.

Into the little mirror above the wash-stand she peered, with smiling and approving eyes. Never had she looked better. There was unusual color, in her cheeks and the clarity of her eyes spoke illuminatingly of superb health. The tan on her face was not made noticeable in contrast by her shoulders and arms, old ivory in tint and as smooth and glossy as ancient Carrara.

"You lovely creature!" murmured Martha, touching an arm with her lips.

"Am I really lovely?"

"You would be adorable if you had a heart."

"Perhaps I have one. Who knows?"

"You are foolish to dress like this." Martha finished the hooking of Elsa's waist.

"And why?"

"In the first place there's nobody worth the trouble; and nobody but a duchess or a . . ." Martha paused embarrassedly.

"Or a what? An improper person?" Elsa laughed. "My dear Martha, your comparisons are faulty. I know but two duchesses in this wide world who are not dowdies, and one of them is an American. An improper person is generally the most proper, outside her peculiar environments. Can't you suggest something else?"

Martha searched but found no suitable reply. One thing she felt keenly, a feverish impatience for the boat to reach Singapore where Elsa's folly must surely end. She believed that she saw more clearly into the future than Elsa. Some one would talk, and in that strange inscrutable fashion scandal has of reaching the ends of the earth, the story would eventually arrive home; and there, for all the professions of friendship, it would find admittance. No door is latched when scandal knocks. Over here they were very far from home, and it was natural that Elsa should view her conduct leniently. Martha readily appreciated that it was all harmless, to be expressed by a single word, whim. But Martha herself never acted upon impulse; she first questioned what the world would say. So run the sheep.

For years Martha had discharged her duties, if mechanically yet with a sense of pleasure and serenity. At this moment she was as one pushed unexpectedly to the brink of a precipice, over which the slightest misstep would topple her. The world was out of joint. Shockingly bad wishes flitted through her head. Each wish aimed at the disposal, imaginary of course, of Warrington: by falling overboard, by being seized with one of the numerous plagues, by having a deadly fracas with one of those stealthy Lascars.

"I wish we had gone to Italy," she remarked finally.

"It would not have served my purpose in the least. I should have been dancing and playing bridge and going to operas. I should have had no time for thinking."

"Thinking!" Martha elevated her brows with an air that implied that she greatly doubted this statement.

"Yes, thinking. It is not necessary that I should mope and shut myself up in a cell, Martha, in order to think. I have finally come to the end of my doubts, if that will gratify you. From now on you may rely upon one thing, to a certainty."

Martha hesitated to put the question.

"I am not going to marry Arthur. He is charming, graceful, accomplished; but I want a man. I should not be happy with him. I can twist him too easily around my finger. I admit that he exercises over me a certain indefinable fascination; but when he is out of sight it amounts to the sum of all this doddering and doubting. It is probable that I shall make an admirable old maid. Wisdom has its disadvantages. I might be very happy with Arthur, were I not so wise." She smiled again at the reflection in the mirror. " Now, let us go and astonish the natives."

There was a mild flutter of eyelids as she sat down beside Warrington and began to chatter to him in Italian. He made a brave show of following her, but became hopelessly lost after a few minutes. Elsa spoke fluently; twelve years had elapsed since his last visit to Italy. He admitted his confusion, and thereafter it was only occasionally that she brought the tongue into the conversation. This diversion, which she employed mainly to annoy her neighbors, was, in truth, the very worst thing she could have done. They no longer conjectured; they assumed.

Warrington was too strongly dazzled by her beauty to-night to be mentally keen or to be observing as was his habit. He never spoke to his neigh-

bor; he had eyes for none but Elsa, under whose
spell he knew that he would remain while he lived.
He was nothing to her; he readily understood.
She was restless and lonely, and he amused her. So
be it. He believed that there could not be an un-
happier, more unfortunate man than himself. To
have been betrayed by the one he had loved, second
to but one, and to have this knowledge thrust upon
him after all these years, was evil enough; but the
nadir of his misfortunes had been reached by the appearance of this unreadable young woman. Of
what use to warn her against himself, or against the
possible, nay, probable misconstruction that would
be given their unusual friendship? Craig would
not be idle with his tales. And why had she put on
all this finery to-night? To subjugate him?

"You are not listening to a word I am saying!"

"I beg your pardon! But I warned you that my
Italian was rusty." He pulled himself together.

"But I have been rattling away in English!"

"And I have been wool-gathering."

"Not at all complimentary to me."

"It is because I am very unhappy; it is because
Tantalus and I are brothers."

"You should have the will to throw off these moods."

"My moods, as you call them, are not like hats and coats."

"I wish I could make you forget."

"On the contrary, the sight of you makes memory all the keener."

He had never spoken like that before. It rather subdued her, made her regret that she had surrendered to a vanity that was without aim or direction. Farthest from her thought was conquest of the man. She did not wish to hurt him. She was not a coquette.

After dinner he did not suggest the usual promenade. Instead, he excused himself and went below.

They arrived at Penang early Monday morning. Elsa decided that Warrington should take her and Martha on a personally conducted tour of the pretty town. As they left for shore he produced a small beautiful blue feather; he gave it to Elsa with the compliments of Rajah; and she stuck it in the pugree of her helmet.

"This is not from the dove of peace."

"Its arch-enemy, rather," he laughed. "I wish I had the ability to get as furious as that bird. It might do me a world of good."

"How long is it since you were here?"

"Four years," he answered without enthusiasm. He would not have come ashore at all but for the fact that Elsa had ordered the expedition.

There was no inclination to explore the shops; so they hired a landau and rode about town, climbed up to the quaint temple in the hills, and made a tour of the botanical gardens.

"Isn't it delicious!" murmured Elsa, taking in deep breaths of the warm spice-laden air. Since her visit to the wonderful gardens at Kandy in Ceylon, she had found a new interest in plants and trees.

She thoroughly enjoyed the few hours on land, even to the powwow Warrington had with the unscrupulous driver, who, at the journey's end, substituted one price for another, despite his original bargain. It was only a matter of two shillings, but Warrington stood firm. It had of necessity become a habit with him to haggle and then to stand firm upon the bargain made. There had been times when half an hour's haggling had meant breakfast or no breakfast. It never entered into his mind what Elsa's point of view might be. The average woman would have called him over-thrifty. All this noise over two shillings! But to Elsa it was only the opening of another door into this strange man's character. What others would have accepted as penuriousness she recognized as a sense of well-balanced justice. Most men, she had found, were afflicted with the vanity of spending, and permitted themselves to be imposed on rather than have others think that money meant anything to them. Arthur would have paid the difference at once rather than have stood on the pier wrangling.

As they waited for the tender that was to convey them back to the ship, Elsa observed a powerful middle-aged man, gray-haired, hawk-faced, steel-eyed, watching her companion intently. Then his boring gaze traveled over her, from her canvas-shoes to her helmet. There was something so baldly appraising in the look that a flush of anger surged into her cheeks. The man turned and said something to his companion, who shrugged and smiled. Impatiently Elsa tugged at Warrington's sleeve.

" Who is that man over there by the railing? " she asked in a very low voice. " He looks as if he knew you."

" Knew me? " Warrington echoed. The moment he had been dreading had come. Some one who knew him! He turned his head slowly, and Elsa, who had not dropped her hand, could feel the muscles of his arm stiffen under the sleeve. He held the stranger's eye defiantly for a space. The latter laughed insolently if silently. It was more for Elsa's sake than for his own that Warrington allowed the other to stare him down. Alone, he would have surrendered to the Berserk rage that urged him to leap across the intervening space and annihilate the man, to crush him with his bare hands until he screamed for the mercy he had always denied others. The flame passed, leaving him as cold as ashes. " I shall tell you who he is later; not here."

For the second time since that night on the Irrawaddy, Elsa recorded a disagreeable sensation. It proved to be transitory, but at the time it served to establish a stronger doubt in regard to her independence, so justifiable in her own eyes. It might be insidiously leading her too far away from the stepping-off place. The unspoken words in those hateful eyes! The man knew Warrington, knew him perhaps as a malefactor, and judged his associates accordingly. She thus readily saw the place she occupied in the man's estimation. She experienced a shiver of dread as she observed that he stepped on board the tender. She even heard him call back to his friend to expect him in from Singapore during the second week in March. But the dread went away, and pride and anger grew instead. All the way back to the ship she held her chin in the air, and from time to time her nostrils dilated. That look! If she had been nearer she was certain that she would have struck him across the face.

"There will be no one up in the bow," said Warrington. "Will you go up there with me?"

After a moment's hesitation, she nodded.

The Lascars, busy with the anchor-chains, demurred; but a word and a gesture from the Sahib who had turned the hose on a drunken man convinced them that the two would not be in the way. A clatter of steel against steel presently followed, the windlass whined and rattled, and Elsa saw the anchor rise slowly from the deeps, bringing up a blur of muddy water; and blobs of pale clay dripped from the anchor-flukes. A moment after she felt the old familiar throb under her feet, and the ship moved slowly out of the bay.

"Do you know that that man came aboard?"

"I know it." The wide half-circle of cocoanut palms grew denser and lower as they drew away. "This is the story. It's got to be told. I should have avoided it if it had been possible. He is the owner of the plantation. Oh, I rather expected something like this. It's my run of luck. I was just recovering from the fever. God knows how he found out, but he did. It was during the rains. He told me to get out that night. Didn't care whether I died on the road or not. I should have but for my boy James. The man sent along with us a poor discarded woman, of whom he had grown tired. She died when we reached town. I had hardly any money. He refused to pay me for the last two months, about fifty pounds. There was no redress for me. There was no possible way I could get back at him. Miss Chetwood, I took money that did not belong to me. It went over gaming-tables. Craig. I ran away. Craig knows and this man Mallow knows. Can you not see the wisdom of giving me a wide berth?"

"Oh, I am sorry!" she cried.

"Thanks. But you see: I am an outcast. To-night, not a soul on board will be in ignorance of who I am and what I have done. Trust Craig and Mallow for that. Thursday we shall be in Singapore. You must not speak to me again. Give them to understand that you have found me out, that I imposed on your kindness."

"That I will not do."

"Act as you please. There are empty chairs at the second-class table, among the natives. And now, good-by. The happiest hours in ten long years are due to you." He took off his helmet and stepped aside for her to pass. She held out her hand, but he shook his head. "Don't make it harder for me."

"Mr. Warrington, I am not a child!"

"To me you have been the Angel of Kindness; and the light in your face I shall always see. Please go now."

"Very well." A new and unaccountable pain

167

filled her throat and forced her to carry her head high. "I can find my way back to the other deck."

He saw her disappear down the first ladder, reappear up the other, mingle with the passengers and vanish. He then went forward to the prow and stared down at the water, wondering if it held rest or pain or what.

XII

D URING the concluding days of the voyage Elsa had her meals served on deck. She kept Martha with her continually, promenaded only early in the morning and at night while the other passengers were at dinner. This left a clear deck. She walked quickly, her arm in Martha's, literally propelling her along, never spoke unless spoken to, and then answered in monosyllables. Her thoughts flew to a thousand and one things: home, her father, episodes from school-life; toward anything and everywhere like a land-bird lost at sea, futilely and vainly in the endeavor to shut out the portrait of the broken man. In the midst of some imaginary journey to the Sabine Hills she would find herself asking: What was he doing, of what was he thinking, where would he go and what would he do? She hated night which, no longer offering sleep, provided nothing in lieu of it, and compelled her to remain in the stuffy cabin. She was afraid.

Early Wednesday morning she passed Craig and Mallow; but the two had wit enough to step aside for her and to speak only with their eyes. She filled Craig with unadulterated fear. Never had he met a woman such as this one. He warned Mallow at the beginning, without explaining in detail, that she was fearless and dangerous. And, of course, Mallow laughed and dragged along the gambler whenever he found a chance to see Elsa at close range.

"There's a woman. Gad! that beach-comber has taste."

"I tell you to look out for her," Craig warned again. "I know what I'm talking about."

"What's she done; slapped your face?"

"That kind of woman doesn't slap. Damn it, Mallow, she rammed a hat-pin into me, if you will know! Keep out of her way."

Mallow whistled. "Oho! You probably acted like a fool. Drinking?"

Craig nodded affirmatively.

"Thought so. Even a Yokohama bar-maid will fight shy of a boozer. I'm going to meet her when we get to Singapore, or my name's not Mallow."

Craig laughed with malice. "I hope she sticks

the pin into your throat. It will take some of the brag out of you. Think because you've got picturesque gray hair and are as strong as a bull, that all the women are just pining for you. Say, let's go aft and hunt up the chap. I understand he's taken up quarters in the second-cabin."

" Doesn't want to run into me. All right; come on. We'll stir him up a little and have some fun."

They found Warrington up in the stern, sitting on the deck, surrounded by squatting Lascars, some Chinamen and a solitary white man, the chief engineer's assistant. The center of interest was Rajah, who was performing his tricks. Among these was one that the bird rarely could be made to perform, the threading of beads. He despised this act as it entailed the putting of a blunt needle in his beak. He flung it aside each time Warrington handed it to him. But ever his master patiently returned it. At length, recognizing that the affair might be prolonged indefinitely, Rajah put two beads on the thread and tossed it aside. The Lascars jabbered, the Chinamen grinned, and the chief engineer's assistant swore approvingly.

" How much'll you take for him? "

171

" He's not for sale," answered Warrington.

The parrot shrilled and waddled back to his cage.

" Fine business for a whole man ! "

Warrington looked up to meet the cynical eyes of Mallow. He took out his cutty and fired it. Otherwise he did not move nor let his gaze swerve. Mallow, towering above him, could scarcely resist the temptation to stir his enemy with the toe of his boot. His hatred for Warrington was not wholly due to his brutal treatment of him. Mallow always took pleasure in dominating those under him by fear. Warrington had done his work well. He had always recognized Mallow as his employer, but in no other capacity: he had never offered to smoke a pipe with him, or to take a hand at cards, or split a bottle. It had not been done offensively; but in this attitude Mallow had recognized his manager's disapproval of him, an inner consciousness of superiority in birth and education. He had with supreme satisfaction ordered him off the plantation that memorable night. Weak as the man had been in body, there had been no indication of weakness in spirit.

Occultly Warrington read the desire in the

other's eyes. " I shouldn't do it, Mallow," he said. " I shouldn't. Nothing would please me better than to have a good excuse to chuck you over the rail. Upon a time you had the best of me. I was a sick man then. I'm in tolerable good health at present."

" You crow, I could break you like a pipe-stem." Mallow rammed his hands into his coat pockets, scowling contemptuously. He weighed fully twenty pounds more than Warrington.

Crow! Warrington shrugged. In the East crow is a rough synonym for thief. " You're at liberty to return to your diggings forward with that impression," he replied coolly. " When we get to Singapore," rising slowly to his height until his eyes were level with Mallow's, " when we get to Singapore, I'm going to ask you for that fifty pounds, earned in honest labor."

" And if I decline to pay? " truculently.

" We'll talk that over when we reach port. Now," roughly, " get out. · There won't be any baiting done to-day, thank you."

The chief engineer's assistant, a stocky, muscular young Scot, stepped forward. He knew Mallow.

"If there is, Mr. Warrington, I'm willing to have a try at losing my job."

"Cockalorem!" jeered Mallow. Craig touched his sleeve, but he threw off the hand roughly. He was one of the best rough and tumble fighters in the Straits Settlements. "You thieving beach-comber, I don't want to mess up the deck with you, but I'll cut your comb for you when we get to port."

Warrington laughed insolently and picked up the parrot-cage. "I'll bring the comb. In fact, I always carry it." Not a word to Craig, not a glance in his direction. Warrington stepped to the companionway and went below.

The chief engineer's assistant, whistling *Bide Awee*, sauntered forward.

Craig could not resist grinning at Mallow's discomfiture. "Wouldn't break, eh?"

"Shut your mouth! The sneaking dock-walloper, I'll take the starch out of him when we land! Always had that high and mighty air. Wants folks to think he's a gentleman."

"He was once," said Craig. "No use giving you advice; but he's not a healthy individual to bait. I'm no kitten when it comes to scrapping; but I haven't any desire to mix things with him." The fury of the man who had given him the ducking was still vivid. He had been handled as a terrier handles a rat.

" Bah ! "

" Bah as much as you please. I picked you out of the gutter one night in Rangoon, after roughing it with half a dozen Chinamen, and saved your wad. I've not your reach or height, but I can lay about some. He'll kill you. And why not? He wouldn't be any worse off than he is."

" I tell you he's yellow. And with a hundred-thousand in his clothes, he'll be yellower still."

A hundred thousand. Craig frowned and gazed out to sea. He had forgotten all about the wind-fall. " Let's go and have a peg," he suggested sur-lily.

Immediately upon obtaining her rooms at Raffles Hotel in Singapore (and leaving Martha there to await the arrival of the luggage, an imposing collection of trunks and boxes and kit-bags), Elsa went down to the American Consulate, which had its offices in the rear of the hotel. She walked through the outer office and stood silently at the consul-general's elbow, waiting for him to look up. She was dressed in white, and in the pugree of her helmet was the one touch of color, Rajah's blue feather. With a smile she watched the stubby pen crawl over some papers, ending at length with a flourish, dignified and characteristic. The consul-general turned his head. His kindly face had the settled expression of indulgent inquiry. The expression changed swiftly into one of delight.

"Elsa Chetwood!" he cried, seizing her hands. "Well, well! I am glad to see you. Missed you when you passed through to Ceylon. Good gracious, what a beautiful woman you've turned out to be! Sit down, sit down!" He pushed her into a chair. "Well, well! When I saw you last you were nineteen."

"What a frightful memory you have! And I was going to my first ball. You used the same adjective."

"Is there a better one? I'll use it if there is. You've arrived just in time. I am giving a little dinner to the consuls and their wives to-night, and you will add just the right touch; for we are all a

little gray at the temples and some of us are a trifle
bald. You see, I've an old friend from India in
town to-day, and I've asked him, too. Your appearance evens up matters."

" Oh; then I'm just a filler-in!"

" Heavens, no! You're the most important person of the lot, though Colonel Knowlton . . ."

" Colonel Knowlton!" exclaimed Elsa.

" That's so, by George! Stupid of me. You
came down on the same boat. Fine! You know
each other."

Elsa straightened her lips with some difficulty.
She possessed the enviable faculty of instantly form-
ing in her mind pictures of coming events. The little swelling veins in the colonel's nose were as plain
to her mind's eye as if he really stood before her.
" Have him take me in to dinner," she suggested.

" Just what I was thinking of," declared the un-
suspecting man. " If any one can draw out the
colonel, it will be you."

" I'll do my best." Elsa's mind was full of rol-
licking malice.

Contemplatively he said: " So you've been doing
the Orient alone? You are like your father in that

way. He was never afraid of anything. Your mental make-up, too, I'll wager is like his. Finest man in the world."

"Wasn't he? How I wish he could have always been with me! We were such good comrades. They do say I am like father. But why is it, every one seems appalled that I should travel over here without male escort?"

"The answer lies in your mirror, Elsa. Your old nurse Martha is no real protection."

"Are men so bad, then?"

"They are less restrained. The heat, the tremendous distances, the lack of amusements, are perhaps responsible. The most difficult thing in the world to amuse is man. By the way, here's a packet of letters for you."

"Thanks." Elsa played with the packet, somberly eying the superscriptions. The old disorder came back into her mind. Three of the letters were from Arthur. She dreaded to open them.

"Now, I'll expect you to come to the apartments and have tea at five."

"Be glad to. Only, don't have any one else. I just want to visit and talk as I used to."

THE GAME OF GOSSIP

" I promise not to invite anybody."

" I must be going, then. I'm not sure of my tickets to Hongkong."

" Go straight to the German Lloyd office. The next P. & O. boat is booked full. Don't bother to go to Cook's. Everybody's on the way home now. Go right to the office. I'll have my boy show you the way. Chong! " he called. A bright-eyed young Chinese came in quickly and silently from the other room. " Show lady German Lloyd office. All same quick."

" All light. Lady come."

" Until tea."

In the outer office she paused for a moment or so to look at the magazines and weeklies from home. The Chinese boy, grinning pleasantly, peered curiously at Elsa's beautiful hands. She heard some one enter, and quite naturally glanced up. The newcomer was Mallow. He stared at her, smiled familiarly and lifted his helmet.

Elsa, with cold unflickering eyes, offered his greeting no recognition whatever. The man felt that she was looking through him, inside of him, searching out all the dark corners of his soul. He dropped

179

his gaze, confused. Then Elsa calmly turned to the boy.

"Come, Chong."

There was something in the manner of her exit that infinitely puzzled him. It was the insolence of the well-bred, but he did not know it. To offset his chagrin and confusion, he put on his helmet and passed into the private office. She was out of his range of understanding.

Mallow was an American by birth but had grown up in the Orient, hardily. In his youth he had been beaten and trampled upon, and now that he had become rich in copra (the dried kernels of cocoanuts from which oil is made), he in his turn beat and trampled. It was the only law he knew. He was without refinement, never having come into contact with that state of being long enough to fall under its influence. He was a shrewd bargainer; and any who respected him did so for two reasons, his strength and his wallet. Such flattery sufficed his needs. He was unmarried; by inclination, perhaps, rather than by failure to find an agreeable mate. There were many women in Penang and Singapore who would have snapped him up, had the opporcunity offered, despite the fact that they knew his history tolerably well. Ordinarily, when in Penang and Singapore, he behaved himself, drank circumspectly and shunned promiscuous companions. But when he did drink heartily, he was a man to beware of.

He hailed the consul-general cordially and offered him one of his really choice cigars, which was accepted.

"I say, who was that young woman who just went out?"

The consul-general laid down the cigar. The question itself was harmless enough; it was Mallow's way of clothing it he resented. "Why?" he asked.

"She's a stunner. Just curious if you knew her, that's all. We came down on the same boat. Hanged if I shouldn't like to meet her."

"You met her on board?"

"I can't say that. Rather uppish on the steamer. But, do you know her?" eagerly.

"I do. More than that, I have always known her. She is the daughter of the late General Chetwood, one of the greatest civil-engineers of our time.

When he died he left her several millions. She is a remarkable young woman, a famous beauty, known favorably in European courts, and I can't begin to tell you how many other accomplishments she has."

"Well, stump me!" returned Mallow. "Is that all straight?"

"Every word of it," with a chilliness that did not escape a man even so impervious as Mallow.

"Is she a free-thinker?"

"What the devil is that? What do you mean?"

"Only this, if she's all you say she is, why does she pick out an absconder for a friend, a chap who dare not show his fiz in the States? I heard the tale from a man once employed in his office back in New York. A beach-comber, a dock-walloper, if there ever was one."

"Mallow, you'll have to explain that instantly."

"Hold your horses, my friend. What I'm telling you is on the level. She's been hobnobbing with the fellow all the way down from the Irrawaddy, so I'm told. Never spoke to any one else. Made him sit at her side at table and jabbered Italian at him, as if she didn't want others to know what she was talking about. I know the man. Fired him from my

plantation, when I found out what he was. Can't
recall his name just now, but he is known out here
as Warrington; Parrot & Co."

The consul-general was genuinely shocked.

"You can't blame me for thinking things," went
on Mallow. "What man wouldn't? Ask her
about Warrington. You'll find that I'm telling the
truth, all right."

"If you are, then she has made one of those mistakes women make when they travel alone. I shall
see her at tea and talk to her. But I do not thank
you, Mallow, for telling me this. A finer, loyaler-
hearted girl doesn't live. She might have been kind
out of sympathy."

Mallow bit off the tip of his cigar. "He's a
handsome beggar, if you want to know."

"I resent that tone. Better drop the subject before I lose my temper. I'l have your papers ready
for you in the morning." The consul-general
caught up his pen savagely to indicate that the interview was at an end.

"All right," said Mallow good-naturedly. "I
meant no harm. Just naturally curious. Can't
blame me."

"I'm not blaming you. But it has disturbed me, and I wish to be alone to think it over."

Mallow lounged out, rather pleased with himself. His greatest pleasure in life was in making others uncomfortable.

The consul-general bit the wooden end of his pen and chewed the splinters of cedar. He couldn't deny that it was like Elsa to pick up some derelict for her benefactions. But to select a man who was probably wanted by the American police was a frightful misfortune. Women had no business to travel alone. It was all very well when they toured in parties of eight or ten; but for a charming young woman like Elsa, attended by a spinster companion who doubtless dared not offer advice, it was decidedly wrong. And thereupon he determined that her trip to Yokohama should find her well guarded.

"I beg your pardon," said a pleasant voice.

The consul-general had been so deeply occupied by his worry that he had not noticed the entrance of the speaker. He turned impatiently. He saw a tall blond man, bearded and tanned, with fine clear blue eyes that met his with the equanimity of the fearless.

XIII

THE consul-general had, figuratively, a complete assortment of masks, such as any thorough play-actor might have, in more or less constant demand, running the gamut from comedy to tragedy. Some of these masks grew dusty between ships, but could quickly be made presentable. Sometimes, when large touring parties came into port, he confused his masks, being by habit rather an absentminded man. But he possessed a great fund of humor, and these mistakes gave him laughable recollections for days.

He saw before him an exquisite, as the ancient phrase goes, backed by no indifferent breed of manhood. Thus, he believed that here was a brief respite (as between acts) in which the little plastic hypocrisies could be laid aside. The pleasant smile on his high-bred face was all his own.

"And what may I do for you, sir?" He ex-

185

pected to be presented with letters of introduction, and to while away a half-hour in the agreeable discussion of mutual acquaintance.

"I should like a few minutes' private talk with you," began the well-dressed stranger. "May I close the door?" The consul-general, with a sense of disappointment, nodded. The blond man returned and sat down. "I don't know how to begin, but I want you to copy this cablegram and send it under your own name. Here it is; read it."

So singular a request filled the consul-general with astonishment. Rather mechanically he accepted the slip of paper, adjusted his glasses, and read —

"The Andes Construction Company, New York: A former employee of yours wishes to make a restitution of eight thousand dollars, with interest to date. He dares not give his name to me, but he wishes to learn if this belated restitution will lift the ban against his returning to America and resuming his citizenship. Reply collect."

"This is an extraordinary request to make to me, sir."

"I know it."

"But why bring it to me?"

"Could I possibly offer that to the cable operator? Without name or address? No; I could not do it without being subjected to a thousand questions, none of which I should care to answer. So I came to you. Passing through your hands, no one will question it. Will you do this favor for a poor unfortunate devil?"

Oddly enough, the other could not get away from his original impression. The clothes, the way the man wore them, the clarity of his eyes, the abundant health that was expressed by the tone of the skin, derided such a possibility as the cablegram made manifest.

He forced the smile back to his lips. "Are you sure you're not hoaxing me?"

"No. I am the victim of the hoax," enigmatically. "If one may call the quirks of fate by the name of hoax," the stranger added. "Will you send it?"

The years he had spent in the consular service had never brought before him a situation of this order. He did not know exactly what to do. He looked out of the window, into the hotel-court, at the sky which presently would become overcast with the daily rain-clouds. By and by he remembered the man waiting patiently at his elbow.

187

" What is your name? "

" My real name, or the one by which I am known here? "

" Your real one."

" I'd rather not give that until I hear from New York."

" Well, that is reasonable."

" I am known out here by the name of Warrington."

Warrington. The puzzlement vanished from the older man's face, and his eyes became alert, renewing from another angle their investigation of the stranger. Warrington. So this was the man? He could understand now. Who could blame a girl for making a mistake when he, a seasoned veteran, had been beguiled by the outward appearance of the man? Mallow was right. He was a handsome beggar.

" I promise to send this upon one condition."

" I accept without question," readily.

" It is that you must keep away from Elsa Chetwood, now and hereafter. You made her acquaintance under false pretenses."

" I deny that. Not under false pretenses." How

188

quickly things went about! "Let me tell you how I met her."

The consul-general listened; he listened with wonder and interest, and more, with conviction that the young man had been perfectly honest. But the knowledge only added to his growing alarm. It would not be difficult for such a man to win the regard of any young woman.

"And you told her what you had done?"

"Yes."

"Your first misstep?" touching the cablegram.

"My first and only misstep. I was a careless, happy-go-lucky young fool." The sky outside also had attraction for Warrington. A thousand times a fool!

"How long ago did this happen?"

"Ten years this coming April."

"And now, after all this time, you wish to go back?"

"I have wished to go back many times, but never had money enough. I have plenty now. Oh, I made it honestly," smiling. "In oil, at Prome. Here's a cutting from a Rangoon paper."

The other read it carefully. It was romance, romance such as he liked to read in his books, but which was mighty bewildering to have at his elbow in actuality. What a life the man must have led! And here he was, with no more evidence of the conflict than might be discerned in the manliness of his face and the breadth and depth of his shoulders. He dropped the cutting, impatiently.

" Don't you believe it? "

" Believe it? Oh, this? Yes," answered the consul-general. " What I can not believe is that I am awake. I can not quite make two and two equal four."

" Which infers? "

" That I can not . . . Well, you do not look like a man who would rob his employer of eight thousand dollars."

" Much obliged."

" Parrot & Co. It's odd, but I recollect that title. You were at Udaipur during the plague."

Warrington brightened. " So that's got about? I happened to be there, working on the prince's railway."

" I will send the cable at once. You will doubtless hear from New York in the morning. But you must not see Miss Chetwood again."

"You will let me bid her good-by? I admire and respect her more than any other woman. She does not know it, for as yet her soul is asleep; but she is one of those few women God puts on earth for the courage and comfort of man. Only to say good-by to her. Here in this office, if you wish."

"I agree to that."

"Thank you again." Warrington rose.

"I am genuinely sorry for you. If they say no, what will you do?"

"Go back just the same. I have another debt to cancel."

"Call in the morning. I'll let you know what the charges are."

"I forgot. Here are twenty pounds. You can return the balance when I call. I am very grateful."

"By the way, there is a man here by the name of Mallow," began the consul-general.

"Yes," interrupted Warrington, with a smile which was grim and cruel. "I expect to call upon

him. He owes me something like fifty pounds, and
I am going to collect it."   Then he went out.

The consul-general dropped Mallow's perfecto
into the waste-basket and lighted his pipe.   Once
more he read the cablegram.   The Andes Construction Company.   What a twist, what an absurd kink
in the skein!   Nearly all of Elsa's wealth lay bound
up in this enormous business which General Chetwood had founded thirty odd years before.   And
neither of them knew!

"I am not a bad man at heart," he mused, "but
I liked the young man's expression when I mentioned that bully Mallow."

He joined his family at five.   He waved aside
tea, and called for a lemon-squash.

"Elsa, I am going to give you a lecture."

"Didn't I tell you?" cried Elsa to the wife.   "I
felt in my bones that he was going to say this very
thing."   She turned to her old-time friend.   "Go
on; lecture me."

"In the first place, you are too kind-hearted."

"That will be news to my friends.   They say I
have a heart of ice."

AFTER TEN YEARS

" And what you think is independence of spirit is sometimes indiscretion."

" Oh," said Elsa, becoming serious.

" A man came into my office to-day. He is a rich copra-grower from Penang. He spoke of you. You passed him on going out. If I had been twenty years younger I'd have punched his ugly head. His name is Mallow, and he's not a savory chap."

Elsa's cheeks burned. She never would forget the look in that man's eyes. The look might have been in other men's eyes, but conventionality had always veiled it; she had never seen it before.

" Go on; " but her voice was unsteady.

" Somewhere along the Irrawaddy you made the acquaintance of a young man who calls himself Warrington, familiarly known as Parrot & Co. I'll be generous. Not one woman in a thousand would have declined to accept the attentions of such a man. He is cultivated, undeniably good-looking, a strong man, mentally and physically."

Elsa's expression was now enigmatical.

" There's not much veneer to him. He fooled me unintentionally. He was quite evidently born a gentleman, of a race of gentlemen. His is not an isolated case. One misstep, and the road to the devil."

The consul-general's wife sent a startled glance at Elsa, who spun her sunshade to lighten the tension of her nerves.

"He confessed frankly to me this morning that he is a fugitive from justice. He wishes to return to America. He recounted the circumstances of your meeting. To me the story appeared truthful enough. He said that you sought the introduction because of his amazing likeness to the man you are going home to marry."

"That is true," replied Elsa. "Uncle Jim, I have traveled pretty much over this world, and I never met a gentleman if Warrington is not one." There was unconscious belligerency in her tone.

"Ah, there's the difficulty which women will never be made to understand. Every man can, at one time or another, put himself upon his good behavior. Underneath he may be a fine rascal."

"Not this one," smiling. "He warned me against himself a dozen times, but that served to make me stubborn. The fault of my conduct,"

acidly, " was not in making this pariah's acquaintance. It lies in the fact that I had nothing to do
with the other passengers, from choice. That is
where I was indiscreet. But why should I put myself out to gain the good wishes of people for whom
I have no liking; people I shall probably never see
again when I leave this port? "

" You forget that some of them will be your fellow passengers all the way to San Francisco. My
child, you know as well as I do that there are some
laws which the Archangel Michael would have to
obey, did he wish to inhabit this earth for a while."

" Poor Michael! And if you do not obey these
laws, people talk."

" Exactly. There are two sets of man-made laws.
One governs the conduct of men and the other the
conduct of women."

" And a man may break any one of these laws,
twist it, rearrange it to suit his immediate needs.
On the other hand, the woman is always manacled."

" Precisely."

" I consider it horribly unfair."

" So it is. But if you wish to live in peace, you
must submit."

195

"Peace at that price I have no wish for. This man Mallow lives within the pale of law; the other man is outside of it. Yet, of the two, which would you be quickest to trust?"

The consul-general laughed. "Now you are appealing not to my knowledge of the world but to my instinct."

"Thanks."

"Is there any reason why you should defend Mr. Warrington, as he calls himself?"

The consul-general's wife desperately tried to catch her husband's eye. But either he did not see the glance or he purposely ignored it.

"In defending Mr. Warrington I am defending myself."

"A good point."

"My dear friend," Elsa went on, letting warmth come into her voice once more, "my sympathy went out to that man. He looked so lonely. Did you notice his eyes? Can a man look at you the way he does and be bad?"

"I have seen Mallow dozens of times. I know him to be a scoundrel of sorts; but I doubt if bald sunlight could make him blink. Liars have first to overcome the flickering and wavering of the eyes."

" He said that."

" Who, Warrington? " puzzled.

" He said almost the same thing. Would he say that if he were a liar? "

" I haven't accused him of being that. Indeed, he struck me as a truthful young man. But he confessed to me that ten years ago he robbed his employer of eight thousand dollars. By the way, what is the name of the firm your father founded? "

" The Andes Construction Company. Do you think we could find him something to do there? " eagerly. " He builds bridges."

" I shouldn't advise that. But we have gone astray. You ought not to see him again."

" I have made up my mind not to."

" Then pardon me for all this pother. I know what is in your heart, Elsa. You want to help the poor devil back to what he was; but he'll have to do that by himself."

" It is a hateful world! " Elsa appealed to the wife.

" It is, Elsa, dear. But James is right."

" You'll get your balance," said the guardian,

"when you reach home. When's the wedding?"

"I'm not sure that I'm going to be married." Elsa twirled the sunshade again. "I really wish I had stayed at home. I seem all topsy-turvy. I could have screamed when I saw the man standing on the ledge above the boat that night. No; I do not believe I shall marry. Fancy marrying a man and knowing that his ghost was at the same time wandering about the earth!" She rose and the sunshade described a half-circle as she spoke. "Oh, bother with it all! Dinner at eight, in the big dining-room."

"Yes. But the introductions will be made on the café-veranda. These people out here have gone mad over cock-tails. And look your best, Elsa. I want them to see a real American girl to-night. I'll have some roses sent up to you."

Elsa had not the heart to tell him that all interest in his dinner had suddenly gone from her mind; that even the confusion of the colonel no longer appealed to her bitter malice. She knew that she was going to be bored and miserable. Well, she had promised. She would put on her best gown; she would talk and laugh and jest be-cause she had done these things many times when her heart was not in the play of it.

When she was gone, the consul-general's wife said: " Poor girl ! "

Her husband looked across the room interestedly. " Why do you say that ? "

" I am a woman."

" That phrase is the City of Refuge. All women fly to it when confronted by something they do not understand."

" Oh, but I do understand. And that's the pity of it."

XIV

ACCORDING TO THE RULES

ELSA sought the hotel rickshaw-stand, selected a sturdy coolie, and asked to be run to the botanical gardens and back. She wanted to be alone, wanted breathing-space, wanted the breeze to cool her hot cheeks. For she was angry at the world, angry at the gentle consul-general, above all, angry at herself. To have laid herself open to the charge of indiscretion! To have received a lecture, however kindly intended, from the man she loved and respected next to her father! To know that persons were exchanging nods and whispers behind her back!

It was a detestable world. It was folly to be honest, to be kind, to be individual, to have likes and dislikes, unless these might be regulated by outsiders. Why should she care what people said? She did not care. What made her furious was the absolute stupidity of their deductions. She had not been indiscreet; she had been merely kindly and human; and if they wanted to twist and misconstrue her actions, let them do so.

She hated the word " people." It seemed to signify all the useless inefficient persons in the world, massed together after the manner of sheep and cattle, stupidest of beasts, always wanting something and never knowing what; not an individual among them. And they expected her to conform with their ways! Was it necessary for her to tell these meddlers why she had sought the companionship of a self-admitted malefactor? . . . Oh, that could not be! If evil were to be found in such a man, then there was no good anywhere. What was one misstep? Was it not written that all of us should make one or more? And surely this man had expiated his. Ten years in this wilderness, ten long lonely years. How many men would have stood up against the temptations of this exile? Few, if any, among the men she knew. And they criticized her because she was sorry for the man. Must she say to them: " Dear people, I spoke to this man and engaged his companionship because I was sorry for him; because he looked exactly like the man I have promised to marry!" It was ridiculous. She laughed. The dear people!

Once or twice she saw inwardly the will-o'-the-wisp lights of her soul. But resolutely she smothered the sparks and bolstered up the pitiful lie.

The coolie stopped suddenly.

"Go on," she said.

But the coolie smiled and wiped his shaven poll. Elsa gazed at the hotel-veranda in bewilderment. Slowly she got out of the rickshaw and paid the fare. She had not the slightest recollection of having seen the gardens. More than this, it was a quarter to seven. She had been gone exactly an hour.

"Perhaps, after all," she thought, "I am hopeless. They may be right; I ought to have a guardian. I am not always accountable for what I do."

She dressed leisurely and with calculation. She was determined to convince every one that she was a beautiful woman, above suspicion, above reproach. The spirit within her was not, however, in direct accord with this determination. Malice stirred into life again; and she wanted to hurt some one, hurt deeply. It was only the tame in spirit who, when injured, submitted without murmur or protest. And Elsa, only dimly aware of it, was mortally hurt.

"Elsa," said Martha, "that frown will stay there some day, and never go away."

Elsa rubbed it out with her finger. "Martha, do you recall that tiger in the cage at Jaipur? How they teased him until he lost his temper and came smashing against the bars? Well, I sympathize with that brute. He would have been peaceful enough had they let him be. Has Mr. Warrington called to-day?"

"No."

"Well, if he calls to-morrow, say that I am indisposed."

Martha evinced her satisfaction visibly. The frown returned between Elsa's eyes and remained there until she went down-stairs to join the consul-general and his wife. She found some very agreeable men and women, and some of her natural gaiety returned. At a far table on the veranda she saw Craig and Mallow in earnest conversation.

She nodded pleasantly to the colonel as the head boy came to announce that dinner was served. Anglo-Indian society had so many twists and ramifications that the situation was not exactly new to the old soldier. True, none had confronted him identical to this. But he had not disciplined men all these years without acquiring abundant self-control. The little veins in his nose turned purple, as Elsa prophesied they would, but there was no other indication of how distasteful the moment was to him. He would surely warn the consul-general, who doubtless was innocent enough.

They sat down. The colonel blinked. " Fine passage we had coming down."

" Was it? " returned Elsa innocently.

The colonel reached for an olive and bit into it savagely. He was no fool. She had him at the end of a blind-alley, and there he must wait until she was ready to let him go. She could harry him or pretend to ignore him, as suited her fancy. He was caught. Women, all women, possessed at least one attribute of the cat. It was digging in the claw, hanging by it, and boredly looking about the world to see what was going on. At that moment the colonel recognized the sting of the claw.

Elsa turned to her right and engaged the French consul discursively: the vandalism in the gardens at

ACCORDING TO THE RULES

Versailles, the glut of vehicles in the Bois at Paris,
the disappearing of the old landmarks, the old Hotel
de Sevigne, now the most interesting *musée* in
France. Indeed, Elsa gradually became the center
of interest; she drew them intentionally. She
brought a touch of home to the Frenchman, to the
German, to the Italian, to the Spaniard; and the
British official, in whose hands the civil business of
the Straits Settlements rested, was charmed to learn
that Elsa had spent various week-ends at the home
of his sister in Surrey.

And when she admitted that she was the daughter of General Chetwood, the man to whom the Indian government had cause to be grateful, upon
more than one occasion, for the solidity of his struc-
tures, the colonel realized definitely the seriousness
of his crucifixion. He sat stiffer and stiffer in his
chair, and the veins in his nose grew deeper and
deeper in hue. He saw clearly that he would never
understand American women. He had committed
an outrageous blunder. He, instead of dominating,
had been dominated by three faultfinding old
women; and, without being aware of the fact, had
looked at things from their point of view. A most

inconceivable blunder. He would not allow that he was being swayed less by the admission of his unpardonable rudeness on board than by the immediate knowledge that Elsa was known to the British official's sister, a titled lady who stood exceedingly high at court.

"Miss Chetwood," he said, lowering his voice for her ears only.

Elsa turned, but with the expression that signified that her attention was engaged elsewhere.

"Yes?"

"I am an old man. I am sixty-two; and most of these sixty-two I have lived roughly; but I am not too old to realize that I have made a fool of myself."

Interest began to fill Elsa's eyes.

"It has been said," he went on, keeping the key, "that I am a man of courage, but I find that I need a good deal of that just now. I have been rude to you, and without warrant, and I offer you my humble apologies." He fumbled with his cravat as if it had suddenly tightened. "Will you accept?"

"Instantly." Elsa understood the quality of courage that had stirred the colonel.

ACCORDING TO THE RULES

" Thanks."

But ruthlessly: " I should, however, like your point of view in regard to what you consider my conduct."

" Is it necessary? "

" I believe it would be better for my understanding if you made a full confession." She did not mean to be relentless, but her curiosity was too strong not to press her advantage.

" Well, then, over here as elsewhere in the world there are standards by which we judge persons who come under our notice."

" Agreed. Individuality is not generally understandable."

" By the mediocre, you might have added. That's the difficulty with individuality; it refuses to be harnessed by mediocrity, and mediocrity holds the whip-hand, always. I represent the mediocre."

" Oh, never! " said Elsa animatedly. " Mediocrity is always without courage."

" You are wrong. It has the courage of its convictions."

" Rather is it not stubbornness, wilful refusal to recognize things as they are? "

PARROT & CO.

He countered the question with another. "Supposing we were all individuals, in the sense you mean? Supposing each of us did exactly as he pleased? Can you honestly imagine a more confusing place than this world would be? The Manchurian pony is a wild little beast, an individual if ever there was one; but man tames him and puts to use his energies. And so it is with human individuality. We of the mediocre tame it and harness and make it useful to the general welfare of humanity. And when we encounter the untamable, in order to safeguard ourselves, we must turn it back into the wilderness, an outlaw. Indeed, I might call individuality an element, like fire and water and air."

"But who conquer fire and water and air?" Elsa demanded, believing she had him pocketed.

"Mediocrity, through the individual of this or that being. Humanity in the bulk is mediocre. And odd as it seems, individuality (which is another word for genius) believes it leads mediocrity. But it can not be made to understand that mediocrity ordains the leadership."

ACCORDING TO THE RULES

"Then you contend that in the hands of the stupid lies the balance of power?"

"Let us not say stupid, rather the unimaginative, the practical and the plodding. The stubbornest person in the world is one with an idea."

"Do you honestly insist that you are mediocre?"

"No," thoughtfully. "I am one of those stubborn men with ideas. I merely insist that I prefer to accept the tenets of mediocrity for my own peace and the peace of others."

Elsa forgot those about her, forgot her intended humiliation of the man at her side. He denied that he was an individual, but he was one, as interesting a one as she had met in a very long time. She, too, had made a blunder. Quick to form opinions, swift to judge, she stood guilty with the common lot, who permit impressions instead of evidence to sway them. Here was a man.

"We have gone far afield," she said, a tacit admission that she could not refute his dissertations. This knowledge, however, was not irksome.

"Rather have we not come to the bars? Shall we let them down?"

" Proceed."

" In the civil and military life on this side of the world there are many situations which we perforce must tolerate. But these, mind you, are settled conditions. It is upon new ones which arise that we pass judgment. I knew nothing about you, nothing whatever. So I judged you according to the rules."

Elsa leaned upon her elbows, and she smiled a little as she noted that the purple had gone from his nose and that it had resumed its accustomed rubicundity.

" I go on. A woman who travels alone, who does not present letters of introduction, who . . ."

" Who attends strictly to her own affairs. Go on."

" Who is young and beautiful."

" A sop! Thanks!"

Imperturbably he continued: " Who seeks the acquaintance of men who do not belong, as you Americans say."

" Not men; one man," she corrected.

" A trifling difference. Well, it arouses a disagreeable word, suspicion. For look, there have been examples. It isn't as if yours were an isolated case. There have been examples, and these we apply to such affairs as come under our notice."

"And it doesn't matter that you may be totally wrong?"

His prompt answer astonished her. "No, it does not matter in the least. Simmered down, it may be explained in a word, appearances. And I must say, to the normal mind . . ."

"The mediocre mind."

"To the normal and mediocre mind, appearances were against you. Observe, please, that I did not know I was wrong, that you were a remarkable young woman. My deductions were made from what I saw as an outsider. On the Irrawaddy you made the acquaintance of a man who came out here a fugitive from justice. After you made his acquaintance, you sought none other, in fact, repelled any advances. This alone decided me."

"Then you were decided?" To say that this blunt exposition was not bitter to her taste, that it did not act like acid upon her pride, would not be true. She was hurt, but she did not let the hurt befog her sense of justice. From his point of view the colonel was in no fault. "Let me tell you how very wrong you were indeed."

"Doubtless," he hastily interposed, "you enveloped the man in a cloud of romance."

"On the contrary, I spoke to him and sought his companionship because he was nothing more nor less than a ghost."

"Ah! Is it possible that you knew him in former times?"

"No. But he was so like the man at home; so identical in features and build to the man I expected to go home to marry. . . ."

"My dear young lady, you are right. Mediocrity is without imagination, stupid, and makes the world a dull place indeed. Like the man you expect to marry! What woman in your place would have acted otherwise? And I have made my statements as bald and brutal as an examining magistrate! Instead of one apology I offer a thousand."

"I accept each and all of them. More, I believe that you and I could get on capitally. I can very well imagine the soldier you used to be. I am going to ask you what you know about Mr. Warrington."

" This, that he is not a fit companion for a young woman like yourself; that a detractable rumor follows hard upon his heels wherever he goes. I learned something about him in Rangoon. He is known to the riff-raff as Parrot & Co., and I don't know what else. All of us on shipboard learned his previous history."

" Ah! " She was quite certain of the historian.

" And not from respectable quarters, either."

" If I had been elderly and without physical attractions? " Elsa inquired sarcastically.

" We are dealing with human nature, mediocrity, and not with speculation. It is in the very nature of things to distrust that which we do not understand. You say, old and without physical attractions. Beauty is of all things most drawing. We crowd about it, we crown it, we flatter it. The old and unattractive we pass by. If I had not seen you here to-night, heard you talk, saw in a kind of rebellious enchantment over your knowledge of the world and your distinguished acquaintance, I should have gone to my grave believing that my suspicions were correct. I dare say that I shall make the same mistake again."

" But do not judge so hastily."

" That I promise."

" Did you learn among other things what Mr. Warrington had done? "

" Yes. A sordid affair. Ordinary peculations that were wasted over gaming-tables."

Warrington had told her the truth. At least, the story told by others coincided with his own. But what was it that kept doubt in her mind? Why should she not be ready to believe what others believed, what the man himself had confessed? What was it to her that he looked like Arthur, that he was guilty or innocent?

" And his name? " She wondered if the colonel knew that also.

" Warrington is assumed. His real name is Paul Ellison."

" Paul Ellison." She repeated it slowly. Her voice did not seem her own. The table, the lights, the faces, all receded and became a blur.

XV

A BIT OF A LARK

MALLOW gave Craig one of his favorite cigars. The gambler turned it over and inspected the carnelian label, realizing that this was expected of him. Mallow smiled complacently. They might smoke as good as that at the government-house, but he rather doubted it. Trust a Britisher to know a good pipe-charge; but his selection of cigars was seldom to be depended upon.

"Don't see many of these out here," was Craig's comment, and he tucked away the cigar in a vest pocket.

"They cost me forty-three cents apiece, without duty." The vulgarian's pleasure lies not in the article itself so much as in the price paid for it. On the plantation Mallow smoked Burma cheroots because he really preferred them. There, he drank rye whisky, consorted with his employees, gambled with them and was not above cheating when he had them drunk enough. Away from home, however, he was the man of money; he bought vintage wines when he could, wore silks, jingled the sovereigns whenever he thought some one might listen, bullied the servants, all with the childish belief that he was following the footsteps of aristocracy, hoodwinking no one, not even his kind. " I'm worth a quarter of a million," he went on. " Luck and plugging did it. One of these fine days I'm going to sell out and take a whack at that gay Paris. There's the place to spend your pile. You can't get your money's worth any place else."

Paris. Craig's thought flew back to the prosperous days when he was plying his trade between New York and Cherbourg, on the Atlantic liners, the annual fortnight in Paris and the Grand-Prix. He had had his diamonds, then, and his wallet of yellow-backs; and when he had called for vintage wines and choice Havanas it had been for genuine love of them. In his heart he despised Mallow. He knew himself to be a rogue, but Mallow without money would have been a bold predatory scoundrel. Craig knew also that he himself was at soul too cowardly to be more than despicably bad. He

216

envied Mallow's absolute fearlessness, his frank
brutality, his strength upon which dissipation had as
yet left no mark; and Mallow was easily forty-
five. Paris. He might never see that city again.
He had just enough to carry him to Hongkong and
keep him on his feet until the races. He sent a
bitter glance toward the sea where the moonlight
gave an ashen hue to the forest of rigging. The
beauty of the scene did not enter his eye. His mind
was recalling the luxurious smoke-rooms.

"When you go to Paris, I'd like to go along."

"You've never let on why they sent you hiking
out here," Mallow suggested.

"One of my habits is keeping my mouth shut."

"Regarding your own affairs, yes. But you're
willing enough to talk when it comes to giving away
the other chap."

"You can play that hand as well as I can."
Craig scowled toward the dining-room doors.

"Ha! There they come," said Mallow, as a
group of men and women issued out into the café-
veranda. "By gad! she *is* a beauty, and no mistake. And will you look at our friend, the colonel,
toddling behind her?"

" You're welcome."

" You're a fine lady-killer." Mallow tore the band from a fresh cigar and struck a match.

" I know when I've got enough. If you could get a good look at her when she's angry, you'd change your tune."

Mallow sighed audibly. " Most women are tame, and that's why I've fought shy of the yoke. Yonder's the sort for me. The man who marries her will have his work cut out. It'll take a year or two to find out who's boss; and if she wins, lord help the man! "

Craig eyed the group which was now seated. Two Chinamen were serving coffee and cordials. Mallow was right; beautiful was the word. A vague regret came to him, as it comes to all men outside the pale, that such a woman could never be his. He poured out for himself a stiff peg and drank it with very little soda. Craig always fled, as it were, from introspection.

" Haven't seen the crow anywhere, have you? "

" No, nor want to. Leave him alone."

" Afraid of him, eh? "

" I'm truthful enough to say that I'm damned

afraid of him. Don't mistake me. I'd like to see
him flat, beaten, down and out for good. I'd like
to see him lose that windfall, every cent of it. But
I don't want to get in his way just now."

"Rot! Don't you worry; no beach-comber like
that can stand up long in front of me. He threatened on board that he was going to collect that fifty
pounds. He hasn't been very spry about it."

"I should like to be with you when you meet."

Mallow grinned. " Not above seeing a pal get
walloped, eh? Well, you get a ring-side ticket.
It'll be worth it."

"I don't want to see you get licked," denied
Craig irritably. " All I ask is that you shelve
some of your cock-sureness. I'm not so dead-broke
that I must swallow all of it. I've warned you that
he is a strong man. He used to be one of the best
college athletes in America."

" College! " exploded Mallow. " What the devil
does a college athlete know about a dock-fight? "

" Ever see a game of football? "

" No."

"Well, take it from me that it's the roughest
game going. It's a game where you put your boot

in a man's face when he's not looking. Mallow, they kill each other in that game. And Ellison was one of the best, fifteen years ago. He used to wade through a ton of solid, scrapping, plunging flesh. And nine times out of ten he used to get through. I want you to beat him up, and it's because I do that I'm warning you not to underestimate him. On shipboard he handled me as you would a bag of salt; damn him! He's a surprise to me. He looks as if he had lived clean out here. There's no booze-sign hanging out on him, like there is on you and me."

"Booze never hurt me any."

"You're galvanized inside," said Craig, staring again at Elsa. He wished he knew how to hurt her, too. But he might as well throw stones at the stars.

"How would you like to put one over on this chap Ellison?"

"In what way?"

Mallow smoked for a moment, then touched his breast pocket significantly.

"Not for mine," returned Craig. "Cards are my long suit. I'm no second-story man, not yet."

" I know.   But supposing you could get it without risk? "

" In the first place, the bulk of his cash is tied up in letters of credit."

" Ah, you know that? "

" What good would it do to pinch those?   In Europe there would be some chance, but not here where boats are two weeks apart.   A cable to Rangoon would shut off all drawing.   He could have others made out.   In cash he may have a few hundreds."

" All gamblers are more or less yellow," sneered Mallow.   " The streak in you is pretty wide.   I tell you, you needn't risk your skin.   Are you game to put one over that will cost him a lot of worry and trouble? "

" So long as I can stand outside the ropes and look on."

" He has a thousand pounds in his belt.   No matter how I found out.   How'd you like to put your hand on it if you were sure it would not burn your fingers? "

" I'd like to, all right.   But it's got to be mighty certain.   And the belt must be handed to me by some one else. I've half a wonder if you're not aiming to get rid of me," with an evil glance at his tempter.

" If I wanted to get rid of you, this'd be the way," said Mallow, opening and shutting his powerful hands. " I'm just hungering for a bit of a lark. Come on. A thousand pounds for taking a little rickshaw ride. Ever hear of Wong's? Opium, pearls, oils and shark-fins? "

" No."

" Not many do. I know Singapore like the lines on my hands. Wong is the shrewdest, most lawless Chinaman this side of Canton and Macao. Pipes, pearls and shark-fins. Did you know that the bay out there is so full of sharks that they have to stand on their tails for lack of space? Big money. Wong's the man to go to. Want a schooner rigged out for illicit shell-hunting? Want a man shanghaied? Want him written down missing? Go to Wong."

" See here, Mallow; I don't mind his being beaten up; but what you say doesn't sound good."

" You fool, I don't want him out of the way.

Why should I? But there's that thousand for you and worry for him. All aboard!"

"You don't love Parrot & Co. any more than I do."

"No. I'd sleep better o' nights if I knew he was broken for keeps. Too much red-tape to put the United States after him. How'd you rig him?"

"Faro and roulette. They never tumble. I didn't have anything against him until he ran into me at Rangoon. But he's stepped in too many times since. Is this straight?"

"About lifting his belt? Easy as falling off a log. Leave it to me. His room is on the first gallery, facing southwest. You can chalk it up as revenge. I'll take it on as a bit of good sport. Wong will fix us out. Now look alive. It's after nine, and I'd like a little fun first."

The two left the café-veranda and engaged a pair of rickshaws. As they jogged down the road, Warrington stepped out from behind the palms and moodily watched them until the night swallowed them up. He had not overheard their interesting conversation, nor had he known they were about until they came down the steps together. He ached to follow them. He was in a fine mood for blows. That there were two of them did not trouble him. Of one thing he was assured: somewhere in the dim past an ancestor of his had died in a Berserk rage.

He had been watching Elsa. It disturbed but did not mystify him to see her talking to the colonel. Table-chance had brought them together, and perhaps to a better understanding. How pale she was! From time to time he caught the flash of her eyes as she turned to this or that guest. Once she smiled, but the smile did not lighten up her face. He was very wretched and miserable. She had taken him at his word, and he should have been glad. He had seen her but once again on board, but she had looked away. It was best so. Yet, it was as if fate had reached down into his heart and snapped the strings which made life tuneful.

And to-morrow! What would to-morrow bring? Would they refuse? Would they demand the full penalty? Eight thousand with interest was a small sum to such a corporation. He had often wondered if they had searched for him. Ten years. In the midst of these cogitations he saw the group at the

table rise and break up. Elsa entered the hotel. Warrington turned away and walked aimlessly toward town. For hours he wandered about, seeing nothing, hearing nothing; and it was long past midnight when he sought his room, restless and weary but wide awake. He called for a stiff peg, drank it, and tumbled into bed. He was whirled away into broken dreams. Now he was running down the gridiron, with the old thrill in his blood. With that sudden inconceivable twist of dreams, he saw the black pit of the tramp-steamer and felt the hellheat in his face. Again, he was in the Andes, toiling with his girders over unspeakable chasms. A shifting glance at the old billiard-room in the club, the letter, and his subsequent wild night of intoxication, the one time in his life when he had drunk hard and long. Back to the Indian deserts and jungles. And he heard the shriek of parrots.

The shriek of parrots. He sat up. Even in his dream he recognized that cry. Night or day, Rajah always shrieked when some one entered the room. Warrington silently slid out of bed and dashed to the door which led to the gallery. A body thudded against his. He caught hold. The body was nude to the waist and smelled evilly of sweat and fish-oil. Something whip-like struck him across the face. It was a queue.

Warrington struck out, but missed. Instantly a pair of powerful arms wound about him, bearing and bending him backward. His right arm lay parallel with the invader's chest. He brought up the heel of his palm viciously against the Chinaman's chin. It was sufficient to break the hold. Then followed a struggle that always remained nightmarish to Warrington. Hither and thither across the room, miraculously avoiding chairs, tables and bed, they surged. He heard a ring of steel upon the cement floor, and breathed easier to learn that the thief had dropped his knife. Warrington never thought to call out for help. The old fear of bringing people about him had become a habit. Once, in the whirl of things, his hand came into contact with a belt which hung about the other's middle. He caught at it and heaved. It broke, and the subsequent tinkling over the floor advised him of the fact that it was his own gold. The broken belt, however, brought the fight to an abrupt end. The oily body suddenly slipped away. Warrington beheld a shadow in the doorway; it loomed there a second against the sky-line, and vanished. He ran to the gallery railing, but it was too dark below to discern anything.

He returned to his room, breathing hard, the obnoxious odor of sweat and fish-oil in his nose. He turned on the lights and without waiting to investigate, went into the shower-room and stood under the tepid deluge. Even after a thorough rub-down the taint was in the air. The bird was muttering and turning somersaults.

"Thanks, Rajah, old sport! He'd have got me but for you. Let's see the damage."

He picked up the belt. The paper-money was intact, and what gold had fallen he could easily find. He then took up his vest . . . and dropped it, stunned. The letter of credit for half his fortune was gone. He sank back upon the bed and stared miserably at the fallen garment. Gone! Fifty thousand dollars. Some one who knew! Presently he stood up and tugged at his beard. After all, why should he worry? A cable to Rangoon would stop payments. A new letter could be issued. It would take time, but he had plenty of that.

PARROT & CO.

Idly he reached for the broken cigar that lay at the foot of the bed. He would have tossed it aside as one of his own had not the carnelian band attracted his attention. He hadn't smoked that quality of tobacco in years. He turned it over and over, and it grew more and more familiar. Mallow's!

XVI

FOR some time Warrington sat upon the edge of the bed and studied the cigar, balanced it upon his palm, as if striving to weigh accurately Mallow's part in a scrimmage like this. The copra-grower assuredly would be the last man to give a cigar to a Chinaman. His gifts kept his coolies hopping about in a triangle of cuffs and kicks and pummelings. He had doubtless given the cigar to another white man likely enough, Craig, who, with reckless inebriate generosity, had in turn presented it to the Oriental. Besides, Mallow was rich. What stepping-stones he had used to acquire his initial capital were not perfectly known; but Warrington had heard rumors of shady transactions and piratical exploits in the pearl zone. Mallow, rich, was Mallow disposed of, at least logically; unless indeed it was a bit of anticipatory reprisal. That might possibly be. A drunken Mallow was capable of much, for all that his knowledge of letters of credit might necessarily be primitive.

Pah! The abominable odor of fish still clung. He reached for his pipe and lighted it, letting the smoke sink into his beard.

Yet, Mallow was no fool. He would scarcely take such risk for so unstable and chancely a thing as revenge of this order. Craig? He hadn't the courage. Strong and muscular as he was, he was the average type of gambler, courageous only when armed with a pack of cards, sitting opposite a fool and his money. But, Craig and Mallow together. . . . He slipped off the label. It was worth preserving.

With an unpleasant laugh he began to get into his clothes. Why not? The more he thought of it, the more he was positive that the two had been behind this assault. The belt would have meant a good deal to Craig. There were a thousand Chinese in Singapore who would cut a man's throat for a Straits dollar. Either Mallow or Craig had seen him counting the money on shipboard. It had been a pastime of his to throw the belt on the bunk-blanket and play with the gold and notes; like a child with its Christmas blocks. He had spent hours gloating over the yellow metal and crackly paper which meant a competence for the rest of his years. And Craig or Mallow had seen him.

He looked at his watch; quarter after two. If they were not in their rooms he would have good grounds for his suspicions. He stole along the gallery and down the stairs to the office, just in time to see the two enter, much the worse for drink. Mallow was boisterous, and Craig was sullen. The former began to argue with the night manager, who politely shook his head. Mallow grew insistent, but the night manager refused to break the rules of the hotel. Warrington inferred that Mallow was demanding liquor, and his inference was correct. He moved a little closer, still hidden behind the potted palms.

" All right," cried Mallow. " We'll go back to town for it."

" I've had enough," declared Craig sullenly.

" Yah! A little sore, eh? Well, I can't pour it down your throat."

" Let's cut out booze and play a little hand or two."

" Fine! " Mallow slapped his thigh as he

231

laughed. "Nice bird I'd be for you to pluck. Think of something else. You can hit me on the head when I'm not looking and take my money that way. What do you think I am, anyhow? The billiard-hall is open."

Craig shook his head. When Mallow was argumentative it was no time to play billiards.

"Bah!" snarled Mallow. "Since you won't drink like a man nor play billiards, I'm for bed. And just as the fun was beginning!"

Craig nudged him warningly. Mallow stalked away, and Craig, realizing that the night was done, followed.

Warrington had seen and heard enough. He was tolerably sure. It might have been out of pure deviltry, so far as Mallow was concerned; but Craig had joined in hope of definite profits. A fine pair of rogues! Neither of them should be able to draw against the letter. He would block that game the first thing in the morning. He would simply notify the local banks and cable to Rangoon.

He eyed indecisively the stairs and then glanced toward the brilliant night outside. It would not be possible to sleep in that room again. So he tiptoed out to the café-veranda and dropped into a comfortable chair. He would hunt them up some time during the day. He would ask Mallow for fifty pounds, and he sincerely hoped that Mallow would refuse him. For he was grimly resolved that Mallow should pay for those half-truths, more damning than bald lies. It was due to Mallow that he was never more to see or speak to Elsa. He emptied the ash from his cutty which he stowed away.

The great heart ache and the greater disillusion would not have fallen to his lot had Elsa been frank in Rangoon, had she but told him that she was to sail on the same steamer. He would have put over his sailing. He would have gone his way, still believing himself to be a Bayard, a Galahad, or any other of those simple dreamers who put honor and chivalry above and before all other things.

Elsa! He covered his face with his hands and remained in that position for a long while, so long indeed that the coolies, whose business it was to scrub the tilings every morning at four, went about their work quietly for fear of disturbing him.

Elsa had retired almost immediately after dinner. She endeavored to finish some initial-work on old embroideries, but the needle insisted upon pausing and losing stitch after stitch. She went to bed and tried to concentrate her thoughts upon a story, but she could no more follow a sentence to the end than she could fly. Then she strove to sleep, but that sweet healer came not to her wooing. Nothing she did could overcome the realization of the shock she had received. It had left her dull and bewildered.

The name echoed and reechoed through her mind: Paul Ellison. It should have been an illumination; instead, she had been thrust into utter darkness. Neither Arthur nor his mother had ever spoken of a brother, and she had known them for nearly ten years. Two men, who might be twin-brothers, with the same name: it was maddening. What could it mean? The beautiful white-haired mother, the handsome charming son, who idolized each other; and this adventurer, this outcast, this patient, brave and kindly outcast, with his funny parrakeet, what was he to them and they to him? It must be, it must be! They *were* brothers. Nature, full of amazing freaks as she was, had not perpetrated this

234

one without calling upon a single strain of blood.

She lay back among her pillows, her eyes leveled at the few stars beyond her door, opened to admit any cooling breeze. Her head ached. It was like the computations of astronomers; to a certain extent the human mind could grasp the distances but could not comprehend them. It was more than chance. Chance alone had not brought him to the crumbling ledge. There was a strain of fatalism in Elsa. She was positive that all these things had been written long before and that she was to be used as the key.

Paul Ellison.

She drew from the past those salient recollections of Arthur and his mother: first, the day the two had called regarding the purchase of a house that her father had just put on the market,—a rambling old colonial affair, her own mother's birth-place. Sixteen: she had not quite been that, just free from her school-days in Italy. With the grand air of youth she had betrayed the fact almost instantly, while waiting for her father to come into the living-room.

"Italy!" said Arthur's mother, whom Elsa

235

mentally adopted at once. The stranger spoke a single phrase, which Elsa answered in excellent if formal Italian. This led from one question to another. Mrs. Ellison turned out to be a schoolmate of her mother's, and she, Elsa, had inherited their very room. What more was needed?

The Ellisons bought the house and lived quietly within it. Society, and there was a good deal of it in that small Kentuckian city, society waited for them to approach and apply for admittance, but waited in vain. Mrs. Ellison never went anywhere. Her son Arthur was a student and preferred his books. So eventually society introduced itself. Persons who ignored it must be interesting. When it became known that Mrs. Ellison had been the schoolmate of the beautiful and aristocratic wife of General Chetwood; when the local banker quietly spread the information that the Ellisons were comfortably supplied with stocks and bonds of a high order, society concluded that it could do very well without past history. That could come later.

When her father died, Elsa became as much at home in the Ellison house as in her own. But never, never anywhere in the house, was there indication of the existence of a brother, so like Arthur that under normal conditions it would have been difficult to tell them apart. Even when she used to go up to the garret with Mrs. Ellison, to aid her in rummaging some old trunk, there came to light none of those trifling knickknacks which any mother would have secretly clung to, no matter to what depth her flesh and blood had fallen. Never had she seen among the usual amateur photographs one presenting two boys. Once she had come across a photograph of a smooth-faced youth who was in the act of squinting along the top of an engineer's tripod. Arthur had laughingly taken it away from her, saying that it represented him when he had had ambitions to build bridges.

To build bridges. The phrase awoke something in Elsa's mind. Bridges. She sat up in bed, mentally keen for the first time since dinner. " I have built bridges in my time over which trains are passing at this moment. I have fought torrents, and floods, and hurricanes, and myself."

He was Paul Ellison, son and brother, and they had blotted him out of their lives by destroying all

physical signs of him. There was something in-
human in the deliberateness of it, something unfor-
givable.

They had made no foolish attempt to live under
an assumed name. They had come from New York
to the little valley in order to leave behind the scene
of their disgrace and all those who had known them.
And they had been extremely fortunate. They
were all gently born, Elsa's friends and acquaintances, above ordinary inquisitiveness, and they had
respected the aloofness of the Ellisons. Arthur was
an inveterate traveler. Half the year found him
in Europe, painting a little, writing a little less,
frequenting the lesser known villages in France and
Italy. He let it be understood that he abhorred
cities. In the ten years they had appeared at less
than a dozen social affairs. Arthur did not care
for horses, for hunting, for sports of any kind.
And yet he was sturdy, clear-eyed, fresh-skinned.
He walked always; he was forever tramping off to
the pine-hooded hills, with his painting-kit over his
shoulders and his camp-stool under his arm.
Later, Elsa began to understand that he was a true
scholar, not merely an educated man. He was be-

sides a linguist of amazing facility, a pianist who invariably preferred as his audience his own two ears. Arthur would have been a great dramatist or a great poet, if . . . If what? If what? Ah, that had been the crux of it all, of her doubt, of her hesitance. If he had fought for prizes coveted by mankind, if he had thrown aside his dreams and gone into the turmoil, if he had taken up a man's burden and carried it to success. Elsa, daughter of a man who had fought in the great arena from his youth to his death, Elsa was not meant for the wife of a dreamer.

Paul Ellison. What was his crime in comparison to his expiation of it? He had built bridges, fought torrents, hurricanes, himself. No, he was not a scholar; he saw no romance in the multifarious things he had of necessity put his hand to: these had been daily matter-of-fact occupations. A strange gladness seemed to loosen the tenseness of her aching nerves.

Then, out of the real world about her, came with startling distinctness, the shriek of a parrot. She would have recognized that piercing cry anywhere. It was Rajah. In the next room, and she had not

known that Warrington (she would always know
him by that name) was stopping at the same hotel!
She listened intently. Presently she heard muffled
sounds: a clatter of metal. A few minutes later
came a softer tinkle, scurry of pattering feet, then
silence.

Elsa ran to the door and stood motionless by the
jamb, waiting, ethereally white in the moonshine.
Suddenly upon the gallery pillars flashed yellow
light. She should have gone back to bed, but a
thrill of unknown fear held her. By and by the
yellow light went out with that quickness which
tricks the hearing into believing that the vanishing
had been accompanied by sound. She saw Warrington, fully dressed, issue forth cautiously,
glance about, then pass down the gallery, stepping
with the lightness of a cat.

She returned hastily to her room, threw over her
shoulders a kimono, and went back to the door, hesi-
tating there for a breath or two. She stepped out
upon the gallery. What had roused him at this
time of night? She leaned over the railing and
peered down into the roadway which in daytime was

given over to the rickshaw coolies. She heard the crunch of wheels, a low murmur of voices; beyond this, nothing more. But as the silence of the night became tense once more, she walked as far as Warrington's door, and paused there.

The gallery floor was trellised with moonlight and shadow. She saw something lying in the center of a patch of light, and she stooped. The light was too dim for her to read; so she reentered her own room and turned on the lights. It was Warrington's letter of credit. She gave a low laugh, perhaps a bit hysterical. There was no doubt of it. Some one had entered his room. There had been a struggle in which he had been the stronger, and the thief had dropped his plunder. (As a matter of fact, the Chinaman, finding himself closed in upon, had thrown the letter of credit toward the railing, in hope that it would fall over to the ground below, where, later, he could recover it.) Elsa pressed it to her heart as another woman might have pressed a rose, and laughed again. Something of his; something to give her the excuse to see and to speak to him again. To-morrow she would know; and he would tell her the truth, even as her heart knew it now. For what other reason had he turned away from her that first day out of Rangoon, hurt and broken? Paul Ellison; and she had told him that she was going home to marry his brother!

XVII

NEXT morning, when it became known among the bankers and foreign agencies that a letter of credit for ten thousand pounds had been lost or stolen, there was more than a ripple of excitement. They searched records, but no loss as heavy as this came to light. Add to the flutter a reward of two hundred pounds for the recovery of the letter, and one may readily imagine the scrutinizing alertness of the various clerks and the subsequent embarrassments of peaceful tourists who wished to draw small sums for current expenses. Even the managing director of the Bank of Burma came in for his share of annoyance. He was obliged to send out a dozen cables of notification of the loss, all of which had to be paid out of accrued dividends. Thus Warrington had blocked up the avenues. The marvelous rapidity with which such affairs may be spread broadcast these days is the first wonder in a new epoch of wonders. From Irkoutsh to Aukland, from St. Johns to Los Angeles, wherever a newspaper was published, the news flew. Within twenty-four hours it would be as difficult to draw against that letter as it would be to transmute baser metals into gold.

At half past ten Warrington, apparently none the worse for a sleepless night, entered the private office of the consul-general who, gravely and with studied politeness, handed to him an unopened cablegram.

" I rather preferred to let you open it, Mr. Warrington," he said.

" Still, it might be something of your own," replied Warrington. He noted the lack of cordiality, but with passive regret.

" No cablegram would come to me from the department, especially as the diplomatic-pouch, as we call the mail-bag, arrives Monday. Open it. I wish you good luck," a little more kindly.

" May I sit down? "

" To be sure you may."

The consul-general recovered his pen and pretended to become absorbed in the litter of papers on his desk. But in truth he could see nothing save the young man's face: calm, unmoved, expressing negligent interest in what should be the most vital thing in his existence, next to life. If the man hadn't met Elsa, to her interest and to his own alarm, he would have been as affable as deep in his heart he wanted to be. A minute passed. It seemed to take a very long time. He tried to resist the inclination to turn his head, but the drawing of curiosity was irresistible. What he saw only added to his general mystification. The slip of paper hung pendulent in Warrington's hand; the other hand was hidden in his beard, while his eyes seemed to be studying seriously the medallion in the Kirmanshah. A fine specimen of a man, mused the consul-general, incredibly wholesome despite his ten years' knocking about in this ungodly part of the world. It was a pity. They had evidently refused to compromise.

"Bad news?"

Warrington stood up with sudden and surprising animation in his face. "Read it," he said.

"If Ellison will make restitution in person, yes.
"ANDES."

The consul-general jumped to his feet and held out his hand. " I am glad, very glad. Everything will turn out all right now. If you wish, I'll tell Miss Chetwood the news."

" I was going to ask you to do that," responded Warrington. The mention of Elsa took the brightness out of his face. " Tell her that Parrot & Co. will always remember her kindness, and ask her to forgive a lonely chap for having caused her any embarrassment through her goodness to him. I have decided not to see Miss Chetwood again."

" You are a strong man, Mr. Warrington."

" Warrington? My name is Ellison, Paul Warrington Ellison. After all, I'm so used to Warrington, that I may as well let well enough alone. There is one more favor; do not tell Miss Chetwood that my name is Ellison."

" I should use my own name, if I were you. Why, man, you can return to the States as if you had departed but yesterday. The world forgets quickly. People will be asking each other what it was that you did. Then I shall bid Miss Chetwood good-by for you? "

THE ANSWERING CABLE

"Yes. I am going to jog it home. I want to travel first-class, here, there, wherever fancy takes me. It's so long since I've known absolute ease and comfort. I wish to have time to readjust myself to the old ways. I was once a luxury-loving chap. I sail at dawn for Saigon. I may knock around in Siam for a few weeks. After that, I don't know where I'll go. Of course I shall keep the Andes advised of my whereabouts, from time to time."

"Another man would be in a hurry." It was on the tip of his tongue to tell Warrington what he knew of the Andes Construction Company, but something held back the words, a fear that Warrington might change his mind about seeing Elsa. "Well, wherever you go and whatever you do, good luck go with you."

"There are good men in this world, sir, and I shall always remember you as one of them."

"By the way, that man Mallow; have you met him yet?"

The quizzical expression in his eyes made Warrington laugh. "No."

"I was in hopes . . ." The consul-general paused, but Warrington ignored the invitation to make known his intentions.

He shunted further inquiry by saying: "A letter of credit of mine was stolen last night. I had a tussle in the room, and was rather getting the best of it. The thug slipped suddenly away. Probably hid the letter in his loin-cloth."

"That's unfortunate."

"In a way. Ten thousand pounds."

"Good lord!"

"I have sent out a general stop-order. No one will be able to draw against it. The sum will create suspicion anywhere."

"Have you any idea who was back of the thief? Is there any way I can be of service to you?"

"Yes. I'll make you temporary trustee. I've offered two hundred pounds for the recovery, and I'll leave that amount with you before I go."

"And if the letter turns up?"

"Send it direct to the Andes people. After a lapse of a few weeks the Bank of Burma will reissue the letter. It will simmer down to a matter of inconvenience. The offer of two hundred is honestly made, but only to learn if my suspicions are correct."

"Then you suspect some one?" quickly.

"I really suspect Mallow and a gambler named Craig, but no court would hold them upon the evidence I have. It's my belief that it's a practical joke which measures up to the man who perpetrated it. He must certainly realize that a letter so large will be eagerly watched for."

"I shall gladly take charge of the matter here for you. I suppose that you will eventually meet Mallow?"

"Eventually suggests a long time," grimly.

"Ah . . . Is there . . . Do you think there will be any need of a watch-holder?"

"I honestly believe you would like to see me have it out with him!"

"I honestly would. But unfortunately the dignity of my office forbids. He has gone up and down the Settlements, bragging and domineering and fighting. I have been given to understand that he has never met his match."

"It's a long lane that has no turning. After all," Warrington added, letting go his reserve; "you're the only friend I have. Why shouldn't I tell you that immediately I am going out in search of him, and that when I find him I am going to give him the worst walloping he ever heard tell of. The Lord didn't give me all this bone and muscle for the purpose of walking around trouble. Doesn't sound very dignified, does it? A dock-walloper's idea; eh? Well, among other things, I've been a dock-walloper, a beach-comber by force of circumstance, not above settling arguments with fists, or boots, or staves. No false modesty for me. I confess I've been mauled some, but I've never been whipped in a man to man fight. It was generally a scrap for the survival of the fittest. But I am going into this affair . . . Well, perhaps it wouldn't interest you to know why. There are two sides to every Waterloo; and I am going to chase Mallow into Paris, so to speak. Oh, he and I shall take away pleasant recollections of each other. And who's to care?" with a careless air that deceived the other.

"I don't believe that Mallow will fight square at a pinch."

"I shan't give him time to fight otherwise."

THE ANSWERING CABLE

" I ought not to want to see you at it, but, hang it, I do! "

" Human nature. It's a pleasurable sensation to back up right by might. Four years ago I vowed that some day I'd meet him on equal terms. There's a raft of things on the slate, for he has been unspeakable kinds of a rascal; beating harmless coolies . . . and women. I may not see you again. If the letter of credit turns up, you know what to do with it. I'm keen to get started. Good-by, and thank you."

A hand-clasp, and he was gone.

" I wish," thought the consul-general, " I could have told him about the way the scoundrel spoke of Elsa."

And Warrington, as he sought the café-veranda, wished he could have told the basic truth of his fighting mood: the look Mallow had given Elsa that day in Penang. Diligently he began the search. Mallow and Craig were still in their rooms, doubtless sleeping off the debauch of the preceding night. He saw that he must wait. Luncheon he had in town.

At four o'clock his inquiries led him into the billiard-annex. His throat tightened a little as he discovered the two men engaged in a game of American billiards. He approached the table quietly. Their interest in the game was deep, possibly due to the wager laid upon the result; so they did not observe him. He let Mallow finish his run. Liquor had no effect upon the man's nerves, evidently, for his eyes and stroke were excellent. A miscue brought an oath from his lips, and he banged his cue upon the floor.

"Rotten luck," said Warrington sympathetically, with the devil's banter in his voice.

XVIII

THE BATTLE

MALLOW spun around, stared for a moment, then grinned evilly. "Here's our crow at last, Craig."

"Speaking of birds of ill-repute, the crow passes his admiration to the kite and the vulture." Warrington spoke coolly.

"Hey, boy; the *chit!*" called Mallow.

"No, no," protested Warrington; "by all means finish the game. I've all the time in the world."

Mallow looked at Craig, who scowled back. He was beginning to grow weary at the sight of Warrington, bobbing up here, bobbing up there, always with a subtle menace.

"What's the odds?" said Mallow jovially. "Only twenty points to go. Your shot."

Craig chalked his cue and scored a run of five. Mallow ran three, missed and swore amiably.

Craig got the balls into a corner and finished his string.

"That'll be five pounds," he said.

"And fifty quid for me," added Warrington, smiling, though his eyes were as blue and hard as Artic ice.

"I'll see you comfortably broiled in hell," replied Mallow, as he tossed five sovereigns to Craig. "Now, what else is on your mind?"

Warrington took out the cigar-band and exhibited it. "I found that in my room last night. You're one of the few, Mallow, who smoke them out here. He was a husky Chinese, but not husky enough. Makes you turn a bit yellow; eh, Craig, you white-livered cheat? You almost got my money-belt, but almost is never quite. The letter of credit is being reissued. It might have been robbery; it might have been just deviltry; just for the sport of breaking a man. Anyhow, you didn't succeed. Suppose we take a little jaunt out to where they're building the new German Lloyd dock? There'll be no one working at this time of day. Plenty of shade."

For a moment the click of the balls on the other

tables was the only sound. Craig broke the tableau by reaching for his glass of whisky, which he emptied. He tried to assume a nonchalant air, but his hand shook as he replaced the glass on the tabouret. It rolled off to the floor and tinkled into pieces.

"Nerves a bit rocky, eh?" Warrington laughed sardonically.

"You're screeching in the wrong jungle, Parrot, old top," said Mallow, who, as he did not believe in ghosts, was physically nor morally afraid of anything. "Though, you have my word for it that I'd like to see you lose every cent of your damned oil fluke."

"Don't doubt it."

"But," Mallow went on, "if you're wanting a little argument that doesn't require pencils or voices, why, you're on. You don't object to my friend Craig coming along?"

"On the contrary, he'll make a good witness of what happens."

"The *chit*, boy!" Mallow paid the reckoning. "Now, then, come on. Three rickshaws!" he called.

"Make it two," said Warrington. "I **have** mine."

"All fine and dandy!"

The barren plot of ground back of the dock was deserted. Warrington jumped from his rickshaw and divested himself of his coat and flung his hat beside it. Gleefully as a boy Mallow did likewise. Warrington then bade the coolies to move back to the road.

"Rounds?" inquired Mallow.

"You filthy scoundrel, you know very well that there won't be any rules to this game. Don't you think I know you? You'll have a try at my knee-pans, if I give you the chance. You'll stick your finger into my eyes, if I let you get close enough. I doubt if in all your life you ever fought a man squarely." Warrington rolled up his sleeves and was pleased to note the dull color of Mallow's face. He wanted to rouse the brute in the man, then he would have him at his mercy. "I swore four years ago that I'd make you pay for that night."

"You scum!" roared Mallow; "you'll never be a whole man when they carry you away from here."

"Wait and see."

THE BATTLE

On the way to the dock Warrington had mapped out his campaign. Fair play from either of these men was not to be entertained for a moment. One was naturally a brute and the other was a coward. They would not hesitate at any means to defeat him. And he knew what defeat would mean at their hands: disfigurement, probably.

" Will you take a shilling for your fifty quid? " jeered Craig. He was going to enjoy this, for he had not the least doubt as to the outcome. Mallow was without superior in a rough and tumble fight.

Warrington did not reply. He walked cautiously toward Mallow. This maneuver brought Craig within reach. It was not a fair blow, but Warrington delivered it without the least compunction. It struck Craig squarely on the jaw. Lightly as a cat Warrington jumped back. Craig's knees doubled under him and he toppled forward on his face.

" Now, Mallow, you and I alone, with no one to jump on my back when I'm looking elsewhere! "

Mallow, appreciating the trick, swore foully, and rushed. Warrington jabbed with his left and side-stepped. One thing he must do and that was to keep Mallow from getting into close quarters.

The copra-grower was more than his match in the knowledge of those Oriental devices that usually cripple a man for life. He must wear him down scientifically; he must depend upon his ring-generalship. In his youth Warrington had been a skilful boxer. He could now back this skill with rugged health and a blow that had a hundred and eighty pounds behind it.

From ordinary rage, Mallow fell into a frenzy; and frenzy never won a ring-battle. Time after time he endeavored to grapple, but always that left stopped him. Warrington played for his face, and to each jab he added a taunt. " That for the little Cingalese!" " Count that one for Wheedon's broken knees!" " And wouldn't San admire that? Remember her? The little Japanese girl whose thumbs you broke?" " Here's one for me!" It was not dignified; but Warrington stubbornly refused to look back upon this day either with shame or regret. Jab-jab, cut and slash! went the left. There was no more mercy in the mind back of it than might be found in the sleek felines who stalked the jungles north. Doggedly Mallow fought on, hoping for his chance. He tried every trick he

knew, but he could only get so near. The ring was as wide as the world; there were no corners to make grappling a possibility.

Some of his desperate blows got through. The bezel of his ring laid open Warrington's forehead. He was brave enough; but he began to realize that this was not the same man he had turned out into the night, four years ago. And the pain and ignominy he had forced upon others was now being returned to him. Warrington would have prolonged the battle had he not seen Craig getting dizzily to his feet. It was time to end it. He feinted swiftly. Mallow, expecting a body-blow, dropped his guard. Warrington, as he struck, felt the bones in his hand crack. Mallow went over upon his back, fairly lifted off his feet. He was tough; an ordinary man would have died.

"I believe that squares accounts," said Warrington, speaking to Craig. "If you hear of me in America, in Europe, anywhere, keep away from the places I'm likely to go. Tell him," with an indifferent jerk of his head toward the insensible Mallow, "tell him that I give him that fifty pounds with the greatest good pleasure. Sorry I can't wait."

He trotted back to his rickshaw, wiped the blood
from his face, put on his hat and coat, and ordered
the respectful coolie to hurry back to town. He
never saw Mallow or Craig again. The battle itself became a hazy incident. In life affairs of this
order generally have abrupt endings.

And all that day Elsa had been waiting patiently
to hear sounds of him in the next room. Never
could she recall such long weary hours. Time and
again she changed a piece of ribbon, a bit of lace,
and twice she changed her dress, all for the purpose
of making the hours pass more quickly. She had
gone down to luncheon, but Warrington had not
come in. After luncheon she had sent out for half
a dozen magazines. Beyond the illustrations she
never knew what they contained. Over and over
she conned the set phrases she was going to say
when finally he came. Whenever Martha approached, Elsa told her that she wanted nothing,
that she was head-achy, and wanted to be left alone.
Discreetly Martha vanished.

To prevent the possibility of missing Warrington, Elsa had engaged the room boy to loiter about

down-stairs and to report to her the moment Warrington arrived. The boy came pattering up at
a quarter to six.

" He come. He downside. I go, he come top-
side?"

" No. That will be all."

The boy kotowed, and Elsa gave him a sovereign.

The following ten minutes tested her patience to
the utmost. Presently she heard the banging of a
trunk-lid. He was there. And now that he *was*
there, she, who had always taken pride in her lack
of feminine nerves, found herself in the grip of a
panic that verged on hysteria. Her heart fluttered and missed a beat. It had been so easy to
plan! She was afraid. Perhaps the tension of
waiting all these hours was the cause. With an
angry gesture she strove to dismiss the feeling of
trepidation by walking resolutely to her door. Outside she stopped.

What was she going to say to him? The trem-
bling that struck at her knees was wholly a new
sensation. Presently the tremor died away, but it
left her weak. She stepped toward his door and

knocked gently on the jamb. No one answered. She knocked again, louder.

" Come in! "

" It wouldn't be proper," she replied, with a flash of her old-time self. " Won't you please come out? "

She heard something click as it struck the floor. (It was Warrington's cutty which he had carried for seven years, now in smithereens.) She saw a hand, raw knuckled and bleeding slightly, catch at the curtain and swing it back rattling upon its rings.

" Miss Chetwood? " he said.

" Yes . . . Oh, you've been hurt! " she exclaimed, noting the gash upon his forehead. A strip of tissue-paper (in lieu of court-plaster) lay soaking upon the wound: a trick learned in the old days when razors grew dull over night.

" Hurt? Oh, I ran against something when I wasn't looking," he explained lamely. Then he added eagerly: " I did not know that you were on this gallery. First time I've put up at a hotel in years." It did not serve.

" You have been fighting! Your hand! "

He looked at the hand dumbly. How keen her eyes were.

"I know!"

"You do?" inanely.

"Was it . . . Mallow?"

"Yes."

"Did you . . . whip him?"

"I . . . did," imitating her tone and hesitance. It was the wisest thing he could have done, for it relaxed the nerves of both of them.

Elsa smiled, smiled and forgot the substance of all her rehearsals, forgot the letter of credit, warm with the heat of her heart. "I am a pagan," she confessed.

"And I am a barbarian. I ought to be horribly ashamed of myself."

"But you are not?"

For a moment their eyes drew. Hers were like dark whirlpools, and he felt himself drifting helplessly, irresistibly. He dropped his hands upon the railing and gripped; the illusion of fighting a current was almost real to him. Every fiber in his body cried out against the struggle.

"No, not in the least," he said, looking toward

263

the sunset. " Fighting is riff-raff business, and I'm only a riff-raffer at best."

" Rather, aren't you Paul Ellison, brother, twin brother, of the man I said I was going home to marry ? "

How far away her voice seemed ! The throb in his forehead and the dull ache over his heart, where some of the sledge-hammer blows had gone home, he no longer felt.

" Don't deny it. It would be useless. Knowing your brother as I do, who could doubt it ? "

He remained dumb.

" I couldn't understand, just simply couldn't. They never told me ; in all the years I have known them, in all the years I have partly made their home my own, there was nothing. Not a trinket. Once I saw a camera-picture. I know now why Arthur snatched it from my hand. It was you. You were bending over an engineer's tripod. Even now I should have doubted had I not recalled what you said one day on board, that you had built bridges. Arthur couldn't build anything stronger than an artist's easel. You are Paul Ellison."

"I am sorry you found out."

"Why?"

"Because I wanted to be no more than an incident in your life, just Parrot & Co."

"Parrot & Co.!"

It was like a caress; but he was too dull to sense it, and she was unconscious of the inflection. The burning sunshine gave to his hair and beard the glistening of ruddy gold. Her imagination, full of unsuspected poetry at this moment, clothed him in the metals of a viking. There were other whirlpools beside those in her eyes, but Elsa did not sense the drifting as he had done. It was insidious.

"An incident," she repeated.

"Could I be more?" with sudden fierceness. "Could I be more in any woman's life? I take myself for what I am, but the world will always take me for what I have done. Yes, I am Paul Ellison, forgotten, I hope, by all those who knew me. Why did you seek me that night? Why did you come into my life to make bitterness become despair? The blackest kind of despair? Elsa Chetwood, Elsa! . . . Well, the consul is right. I *am* a strong man. I can go out of your life, at least physically. I can say that I love you, and I can add to that good-by!"

He wheeled abruptly and went quickly down the gallery, bareheaded, without any destination in his mind, with only one thought, to leave her before he lost the last shreds of his self-control.

It was then that Elsa knew her heart. She had spoken truly. She was a pagan: for, had he turned and held out his hands, she would have gone to him, gone with him, anywhere in the world, lawfully or unlawfully.

XIX

TWO LETTERS

ELSA sang. She flew to her mirror. The face
was hers and yet not hers. Always her mirror had told her that she was beautiful; but up to
this moment her emotion had recorded nothing
stronger than placid content. Now a supreme gladness filled and tingled her because her beauty was
indisputable. When Martha came to help her dress
for dinner, she still sang. It was a wordless song,
a melody that every human heart contains and which
finds expression but once. Elsa loved.

Doubt, that arch-enemy of love and faith and
hope, doubt had spread its dark pinions and flown
away into yesterdays. She felt the zest and exhilaration of a bird just given its freedom. Once she
slipped from Martha's cunning hands and ran out
upon the gallery.

"Elsa, your waist!"

Elsa laughed and held out her bare arms to the

faded sky where, but a little while since, the sun had burned a pathway down the world. All in an hour, one small trifling space of time, this wonderful, magical thing had happened. He loved her. There had been hunger for her in his voice, in his blue eyes. Presently she was going to make him feel very sorry that he had not taken her in his arms, then and there.

"Oh, beautiful world!"

"Elsa, what in mercy's name possesses you?"

"I am mad, Martha, mad as a March hare, whatever that is!" She loved.

"People will think so, if they happen to come along and see that waist. Please come instantly and let me finish hooking it. You act like you did when you were ten. You never would stand still."

"Yes, and I remember how you used to yank my pig-tails. I haven't really forgiven you yet."

"I believe it's going home that's the matter with you. Well, I for one shall be glad to leave this horrid country. Chinamen everywhere, in your room, at your table, under your feet. And in the streets, Chinamen and Malays and Hindus, and I don't know what other outlandish races and tribes.

268

TWO LETTERS

. . . Why, what's this?" cried Martha, bending to the floor.

Elsa ran back to the room. She gave a little gasp when she saw what it was that Martha was holding out for her inspection. It was Warrington's letter of credit. She had totally forgotten its existence. Across the face of the thick Manila envelope (more or less covered with numerals that had been scribbled there by Warrington in an attempt to compute the interest at six per cent.) which contained the letters of credit and identification was written in a clerical hand the owner's name. Martha could not help seeing it. Elsa explained frankly what it was and how it had come into her possession. Martha was horrified.

" Elsa, they might have entered your room; and your jewels lying about everywhere! How could you be so careless? "

" But they didn't. I'll return this to Mr. Warrington in the morning; perhaps to-night, if I see him at dinner."

" He was in the next room, and we never knew it! " The final hook snapped into place. " Well, Wednesday our boat leaves; " as if this put a period to all further discussion anent Mr. Parrot & Co. Nothing very serious could happen between that time and now.

"Wednesday night." Elsa began to sing again, but not so joyously. The petty things of every-day life were lifting their heads once more, and of necessity she must recognize them.

She sat at the consul-general's table, informally. There was gay inconsequential chatter, an exchange of recollections and comparisons of cities and countries they had visited at separate times; but neither she nor he mentioned the chief subject of their thoughts. She refrained because of a strange yet natural shyness of a woman who has found herself; and he, because from his angle of vision it was best that Warrington should pass out of her life as suddenly and mysteriously as he had entered it. Had he spoken frankly he would have saved Elsa many a bitter heartache, many a weary day.

Warrington was absent, and so were his enemies. If there was any truth in reincarnation, Elsa was confident that in the splendid days of Rome she had beaten her pink palms in applause of the gladiators. Pagan; she was all of that; for she knew that she could have looked upon Mallow's face with more than ordinary interest. Never more would her cheeks burn at the recollection of the man's look.

She was twenty-five; she had waited longer than most women; the mistake of haste would never be hers. Nor did she close her eyes to the future. She knew exactly what the world was, and how it would act. She was not making any sacrifices. She was not one of those women, lightly balanced, who must have excitement in order to exist; she depended upon herself for her amusements. With the man she loved she would have shared a hut in the wilderness and been happy. One of the things that had drawn her to Arthur had been his quiet love of the open, his interest in flowers and forests and streams. Society, that division of classes, she had accepted, but to it she had never bowed down. How very well she could do without it! She would go with him and help him build his bridges, help him to fight torrents and hurricanes, and to forget. That he had bidden her farewell was nothing. She would seek him. In her pursuit of happiness she was not going to permit false modesty to intervene.

In her room, later, she wrote two letters. The

one to Arthur covered several pages; the other consisted of a single line. She went down to the office, mailed Arthur's letter and left the note in Warrington's key-box. It was not an intentionally cruel letter she had written to the man in America; but if she had striven toward that effect she could not have achieved it more successfully. She cried out against the way he had treated his brother, the false pride that had hidden all knowledge of him from her. Where were the charity and mercy of which he had so often preached? Pages of burning reproaches which seared the soul of the man who read them. She did not confide the state of her heart. It was not necessary. The arraignment of the one and the defense of the other were sufficiently illuminating.

Soundly the happy sleep. She did not hear the removal of Warrington's luggage at midnight, for it was stealthily done. Neither did she hear the fretful mutter of the bird as his master disturbed his slumbers. Nothing warned her that he intended to spend the night on board; that, having paid his bill early in the evening, her note might have lain in the key-box until the crack of doom, so far as he was likely to know of its existence. No angel of pity whispered to her, Awake! No dream-magic people tell about drew for her the picture of the man she loved, pacing up and down the cramped deck of the packet-boat, fighting a battle compared to which that of the afternoon was play. Elsa slept on, dreamless.

When she awoke in the morning she ran to the mirror: all this fresh beauty she was going to give to him, without condition, without reservation, absolutely: as Aspasia might have rendered her charms to Pericles. She dressed quickly, singing lowly. Fate makes us the happiest when she is about to crush us.

Usually she had her breakfast served in the room, but this morning she was determined to go downstairs. She was excited; she brimmed with exuberance; she wanted Romance to begin at once.

"Good-morning," she greeted the consul-general, who was breakfasting alone.

"Well, you're an early bird!" he replied. "Elsa, you are certainly beautiful."

"Honestly?" with real eagerness.

"Honestly. And how you have gone all these

years without marrying a grand duke, is something I can't figure out."

"Perhaps I have been waiting for the man. There was no real hurry."

"Lucky chap, when you find him. By the way, our romantic Parrot & Co. have gone."

"Gone?" Elsa stared at him.

"Yes. Sailed for Saigon at dawn."

"Saigon," she repeated.

"And I am rather glad to see him go. I was afraid he might interest you too much. You'll deny it, but you'll never outgrow the fairy-story age."

"Saigon."

"Good heavens, Elsa, what is the matter?"

"No, no! Don't touch me. I'm not the fainting kind. Did you know last night that he was going?"

"Yes."

"I shall never forgive you."

"Why, Elsa . . ."

"Never, never! You knew and did not tell me. Do you know who Paul Ellison is? He is the brother of the man at home. You knew he was stealing away and did not tell me."

TWO LETTERS

She could not have made the truth any plainer to him. He sat back in his chair, stunned, voiceless.

"I am going to my room," she said. "Do not follow. Please act as if nothing had happened."

He saw her walk bravely the length of the dining-room, out into the office. What a misfortune! Argument was out of the question. Elsa was not a child, to be reasoned with. She was a woman, and she had come to a woman's understanding of her heart. To place before her the true angles of the case, the heartless banishment from the world she knew, the regret which would be hers later, no matter how much she loved the man . . . He pushed back his chair, leaving his coffee untasted.

He possessed the deep understanding of the kindly heart, and his one thought was Elsa's future happiness. As men go, Warrington was an honorable man; honorable enough to run away rather than risk the danger of staying where Elsa was. He was no longer an outlaw; he could go and come as he would. But there was that misstep, not printed in shifting sand but upon the granite of recollection.

275

Single, he could go back to his world and pick up the threads again, but not with a wife at his side. Oh, yes; they would be happy at first. Then Elsa would begin to miss the things she had so gloriously thrown away. The rift in the lute; the canker in the rose. They were equally well-born, well-bred; politeness would usurp affection's hold. Could he save her from the day when she would learn Romance had come from within? No. All he could do was to help her find the man.

He sent five cablegrams to Saigon, to the consulate, to the principal hotels: the most difficult composition he had ever attacked. But because he had forgotten to send the sixth to meet the packet-boat, against the possibility of Warrington changing his mind and not landing, his labor was thrown to the winds.

Meantime Elsa stopped at the office-desk. " I left a note for Mr. Warrington who has gone to Saigon. I see it in his key-box. Will you please return it to me?"

The clerk did not hesitate an instant. He gravely returned the note to her, marveling at her paleness. Elsa crushed the note in her hand and moved toward the stairs, wondering if she could reach her room before she broke down utterly. He had gone. He had gone without knowing that all he wanted in life was his for the taking. In her room she opened the note and through blurred vision read what she had so happily inscribed the night before. "Paul — I love you. Come to me. Elsa." She had written it, unashamed.

She flung herself upon the bed, and there Martha found her.

"Elsa, child, what is it?" Martha cried, kneeling beside the bed. "Child, what has happened?"

Elsa sat up, seized Martha by the shoulders and stared into the faithful eyes.

"Do you want to know?"

"Elsa!"

"Well, I love this man Warrington and he loves me. But he has gone. Can't you see? Don't you understand? Have you been as blind as I? He is Paul Ellison, Arthur's brother, his twin brother. And they obliterated him. It is Arthur who is the ghost, Martha, the phantom. Ah, I have caused you a good deal of worry, and I am going to cause you yet more. I am going to Saigon; up and down

the world, east and west, until I find him. Shall I
go alone, or will you go with me?"

Then Martha did what ever after endeared her to
the heart of the stricken girl: she mothered her.
"Elsa, my baby! Of course I shall go with you, always. For you could not love any man if he was
not worthy."

Then followed the strangest quest doubtless ever
made by a woman. From Singapore to Saigon, up
to Bangkok, down to Singapore again; to Batavia,
over to Hongkong, Shanghai, Pekin, Manila, Hongkong again, then Yokohama. Patient and hopeful,
Elsa followed the bewildering trail. She left behind her many puzzled hotel managers and booking
agents: for it was not usual for a beautiful young
woman to go about the world, inquiring for a blond
man with a parrot. Sometimes she was only a day
late. Many cablegrams she sent, but upon her arrival in each port she found that these had not been
called for. Over these heart-breaking disappoint-
ments she uttered no complaint. The world was
big and wide; be it never so big and wide, Elsa knew
that some day she would find him.

In the daytime there was the quest; but, ah! the

nights, the interminable hours of inaction, the spaces of time in which she could only lie back and think. Up and down the coasts, across islands, over seas, the journey took her, until one day in July she found herself upon the pillared veranda of the house in which her mother had been born.

XX

FROM port to port, sometimes not stepping off the boat at all, moody, restless and irritable, Warrington wended his way home. There was nothing surprising in the fact that he never inquired for mail. Who was there to write? Besides, he sought only the obscure hotels, where he was not likely to meet any of his erstwhile fellow passengers. The mockery and uselessness of his home-going became more and more apparent as the days slipped by. Often he longed to fly back to the jungles, to James, and leave matters as they were. Here and there, along the way, he had tried a bit of luxury; but the years of economy and frugality had robbed him of the ability to enjoy it. He was going home . . . to what? Surely there would be no welcome for him at his journey's end. He would return after the manner of prodigals in general, not scriptural, to

280

find that he was not wanted. Of his own free will he had gone out of their lives.

He fought grimly against the thought of Elsa; but he was not strong enough to vanquish the longings from his heart and mind. Always when alone she was in fancy with him, now smiling amusedly into his face, now peering down at the phosphorescence seething alongside, now standing with her chin uplifted, her eyes half shut, letting the strong winds strike full in her face. Many a " good night " he sent over the seas. An incident; that would be all.

His first day in New York left him with nothing more than a feeling of foreboding and oppression. The expected exhilaration of returning to the city of his birth did not materialize. So used to open spaces was he, to distances and the circle of horizons, that he knew he no longer belonged to the city with its Himalayan gorges and cañons, whose torrents were human beings and whose glaciers were the hearts of these. A great loneliness bore down on him. For months he had been drawing familiar pictures, and to find none of these was like coming home to an empty house. The old life was indeed gone; there were no threads to resume. A hotel stood where his club had been; the house in which he had spent his youth was no more. He wanted to leave the city; and the desire was with difficulty overcome.

Early the second morning he started down-town to the offices of the Andes Construction Company. He was extraordinarily nervous. Cold sweat continually moistened his palms. Change, change, everywhere change; Trinity was like an old friend. When the taxicab driver threw off the power and indicated with a jerk of his head a granite shaft that soared up into the blue, Warrington asked: " What place is this? "

" The Andes Building, sir. The construction company occupies the top floor."

"Very good," replied Warrington, paying and discharging the man.

From a reliquary of the Dutch, an affair of red-brick, four stories high, this monolith had sprung. With a sigh Warrington entered the cavernous door-way and stepped into an " express-elevator." When the car arrived at the twenty-second story, Warrington was alone. He paused before the door of the vice-president. He recalled the " old man," thin-lipped, blue-eyed, eruptive. It was all very strange, this request to make the restitution in person. Well he would soon learn why.

He drew the certified check from his wallet and scrutinized it carefully. Twelve thousand, eight hundred dollars. He replaced it, opened the door, and walked in. A boy met him at the railing and briskly inquired his business.

"I wish to see Mr. Elmore."

"Your card."

Card? Warrington had not possessed such a thing in years. "I have no cards with me. But I have an appointment with Mr. Elmore. Tell him that Mr. Ellison is here."

The boy returned promptly and signified that Mr. Elmore was at liberty. But it was not the "old man" who looked up from a busy man's desk. It was the son: so far, the one familiar face Warrington had seen since his arrival. There was no hand-shaking; there was nothing in evidence on either side to invite it.

"Ah! Sit down, Paul. Let no one disturb me for an hour," the young vice-president advised the boy. "And close the door as you go out."

Warrington sat down; the bridge-builder whirled his chair around and stared at his visitor, not insolently, but with kindly curiosity.

"You've filled out," was all he said. After fully satisfying his eyes, he added: "I dare say you expected to find father. He's been gone six years," indicating one of the two portraits over his desk.

It was not at the "old man" Warrington looked longest. "Who is the other?" he asked.

"What? You worked four years with this company and don't recollect that portrait?"

"Frankly, I never noticed it before." Warrington placed the certified check on the desk. "With interest," he said.

The vice-president crackled it, ran his fingers over his smooth chin, folded the check and extended it toward the astonished wanderer.

"We don't want that, Paul. What we wanted was to get you back. There was no other way. Your brother made up the loss the day after you . . . went away. There was no scandal. Only a few of us in the office knew. Never got to the newspapers."

It was impossible for Warrington to digest this

284

astounding information at once. His mind could only repeat the phrases: no scandal, only a few of us in the office knew, never got to the newspapers. For ten years he had hidden himself in wildernesses, avoided hotels, read no American newspapers, never called for mail. Oh, monumental fool!

"And I could have come home almost at once!" he said aloud, addressing the crumpled check in his hand rather than the man in the swivel-chair.

"Yes. I have often wondered where you were, what you were doing. You and your brother were upper-classmen. I never knew Arthur very well; but you and I were chummy, after a fashion. Arthur was a little too bookish for my style. Didn't we use to call you Old Galahad? You were always walloping the bullies and taking the weaker chaps under your wing. To me, you were the last man in the world for this business. Moreover, I never could understand, nor could father, how you *got* it, for you were not an office-man. Women and cards, I suppose. Father said that you had the making of a great engineer. Fierce place, this old town," waving his hand toward the myriad sparkling roofs and towers and spires. "Have to be strong and hard-headed to survive it. Built anything since you've been away?"

"In Cashmir." To have thrown away a decade!

"Glad you kept your hand in. I dare say you've seen a lot of life." To the younger man it was an extremely awkward interview.

"Yes; I've seen life," dully.

"Orient, mostly, I suppose. Your letter about the strike in oil was mighty interesting. Heap of money over there, if they'd only let us smart chaps in to dig it up. Now, old man, I want you to wipe the slate clear of these ten years. We'll call it a bad dream. What are your plans for the future?"

"Plans?" Warrington looked up blankly. He realized that he had made no plans for the future.

"Yes. What do you intend to do? A man like you wasn't made for idleness. Look here, Paul; I'm not going to beat about the bush. We've got a whopping big contract from the Chinese government, and we need a man to take charge, a man who knows and understands something of the yellow people. How about a salary of ten thousand a year for two years, to begin in October?"

THE TWO BROTHERS

Warrington twisted the check. Work, rehabilitation.

" Could you trust me? " he asked quietly.

" With anything I have in the world. Understand, Paul, there's no philanthropic string to this offer. You've pulled through a devil of a hole. You're a man. I should not be holding down this chair if I couldn't tell a man at a glance. We were together two months in Peru. I'm familiar with your work. Do you want to know whose portrait that is up there? Well, it's General Chetwood's, the founder of this concern, the silent partner. The man who knew kings and potentates and told 'em that they needed bridges in their backyards. This building belongs to his daughter. She converted her stock into granite. About a month ago I received a letter from her. It directly concerned you. It seems she learned through the consul-general at Singapore that you had worked with us. She's like her father, a mighty keen judge of human nature. Frankly, this offer comes through her advices. To satisfy yourself, you can give us a surety-bond for fifty thousand. It's not obligatory, however."

Elsa Chetwood. She had her father's eyes, and it was this which had drawn his gaze to the portrait. Chetwood; and Arthur had not known any more than he had. What irony! Ten years wasted . . . for nothing! Warrington laughed aloud. A weakness seized him, like that of a man long gone hungry.

"Buck up, Paul," warned the good Samaritan. "All this kind of knocks the wind out of you. I know. But what I've offered you is in good faith. Will you take it?"

"Yes," simply.

"That's the way to talk. Supposing you go out to lunch with me? We'll talk it over like old times."

"No. I haven't seen . . ."

"To be sure! I forgot. Do you know where they live, your mother and brother?"

"No. I expected to ask you."

The vice-president scribbled down the address. "I believe you'll find them both there, though Arthur, I understand, is almost as great a traveler as you are. Of course you want to see them, you poor beggar! The Southwestern will pull you almost up to the door. After the reunion, you hike back here, and we'll get down to the meat of the business."

"John," said Warrington, huskily, "you're a man."

"Oh, piffle! It's not all John. The old man left word that if you ever turned up again to hang on to you. You were valuable. And there's Miss Chetwood. If you want to thank anybody, thank her." Warrington missed the searching glance, which was not without its touch of envy. "You'd better be off. Hustle back as soon as you can." Elmore offered his hand now. "Gad! but you haven't lost any of your old grip."

"I'm a bit dazed. The last six months have loosened up my nerves."

"Nobody's made of iron."

"I'd sound hollow if I tried to say what I feel. I'll be back a week from to-day."

"I'll look for you."

As the door closed behind Warrington, the young millionaire sat down, scowling at a cubby-hole in his desk. He presently took out a letter postmarked Yokohama. He turned it about in his hands, musingly. Without reading it (for he knew its contents well!) he thrust it back into the cubby-hole. Women were out of his sphere. He could build a bridge within a dollar of the bid; but he knew nothing about women beyond the fact that they were always desirable.

A few monosyllables, a sentence or two, and then, good day. The average man would have recounted every incident of note during those ten years. He did not admire Warrington any the less for his reticence. It took a strong man to hold himself together under all these blows from the big end of fortune's horn.

He had known the two brothers at college, and to Paul he had given a freshman's worship. In the field Paul had been the idol, and popular not only for his feats of strength but for his lovableness. He recalled the affection between the two boys. Arthur admired Paul for his strength, Paul admired and gloried in his brother's learning. Never would he forget that commencement-day, when the two boys in their mortar-boards, their beautiful mother between them, arm in arm, walked across the green of the campus. It was an unforgettable picture.

Paul was a born-engineer; Arthur had entered the

office as a make-shift. Paul had taken eight-thousand one day, and decamped. Arthur had refunded the sum, and disappeared. Elmore could not understand, nor could his father. Perhaps some of the truth would now come to light. Somehow, Paul, with his blond beard and blonder head, his bright eyes, his tan, his big shoulders, somehow Paul was out of date. He did not belong to the times.

And Elsa had met him over there; practically ordered (though she had no authority) that he should be given a start anew; that, moreover, she would go his bond to any amount. Funny old world! Well, he was glad. Paul was a man, a big man, and that was the sort needed in the foreign bridge-building. He rolled down the top of his desk and left the building. He was in no mood for work.

The evening of the third day found Warrington in the baggage-car, feeding a dilapidated feather-molting bird, who was in a most scandalous temper. Rajah scattered the seeds about, spurned the banana-tip, tilted the water-cup and swashbuckled generally. By and by, above the clack-clack of wheels and rails, came a crooning song. The baggage-man looked up from his way-book and lowered his pipe. He saw the little green bird pause and begin to keep time with its head. It was the Urdu lullaby James used to sing. It never failed to quiet the little parrot. Warrington went back to his Pullman, where the porter greeted him with the information that the next stop would be his. Ten minutes later he stepped from the train, a small kitbag in one hand and the parrot-cage in the other.

He had come prepared for mistake on the part of the natives. The single smart cabman lifted his hat, jumped down from the box, and opened the door. Warrington entered without speaking. The door closed, and the coupé rolled away briskly. He was perfectly sure of his destination. The cabman had mistaken him for Arthur. It would be better so. There would be no after complications when he departed on the morrow. As the coupé took a turn, he looked out of the window. They were entering a driveway, lined on each side of which were chestnuts. Indeed, the house was set in the center of a grove of these splendid trees. The coupé stopped.

" Wait," said Warrington, alighting.

" Yes, sir."

Warrington went up the broad veranda steps and

pulled the old-fashioned bell-cord. He was rather amazed at his utter lack of agitation. He was as calm as if he were making a call upon a casual acquaintance. His mother and brother, whom he had not seen in ten years! The great oak-door drew in, and he entered unceremoniously.

"Why, Marse A'thuh, I di'n't see yo' go out!" exclaimed the old negro servant.

"I am not Arthur; I am his brother Paul. Which door?"

Pop-eyed, the old negro pointed to a door down the hall. Then he leaned against the banister and caught desperately at the spindles. For the voice was not Arthur's.

Warrington opened the door, closed it gently and stood with his back to it. At a desk in the middle of the room sat a man, busy with books. He raised his head.

"Arthur, don't you know me?"

"Paul?"

The chair overturned; some books thudded dully upon the rug. Arthur leaned with his hands tense upon the desk. Paul sustained the look, his eyes sad and his face pale and grave.

XXI

HE THAT WAS DEAD

"YES, it is I, the unlucky penny; Old Galahad, in flesh and blood and bone. I shouldn't get white over it, Arthur. It isn't worth while. I can see that you haven't changed much, unless it is that your hair is a little paler at the temples. Gray? I'll wager I've a few myself." There was a flippancy in his tone that astonished Warrington's own ears, for certainly this light mockery did not come from within. At heart he was sober enough.

To steady the thundering beat of his pulse he crossed the room, righted the chair, stacked the books and laid them on the desk. Arthur did not move save to turn his head and to follow with fascinated gaze his brother's movements.

"Now, Arthur, I've only a little while. I can see by your eyes that you are conjuring up all sorts of terrible things. But nothing is going to happen.

HE THAT WAS DEAD

I am going to talk to you; then I'm going away; and to-morrow it will be easy to convince yourself that you have seen only a ghost. Sit down. I'll take this chair at the left."

Arthur's hands slid from the desk; in a kind of collapse he sat down. Suddenly he laid his head upon his arms, and a great sigh sent its tremor across his shoulders. Warrington felt his heart swell. The past faded away; his wrongs became vapors. He saw only his brother, the boy he had loved so devotedly, Arty, his other self, his scholarly other self. Why blame Arthur? He, Paul, was the fool.

"Don't take it like that, 'Arty," he said.

The other's hand stretched out blindly toward the voice. "Ah, great God, Paul!"

"I know! Perhaps I've brooded too much." Warrington crushed the hand in his two strong ones. "The main fault was mine. I couldn't see the length of my nose. I threw a temptation in your way which none but a demi-god could have resisted. That night, when I got your note telling me what you had done, I did a damnably foolish thing. I went to the club-bar and drank heavily. I was wild to help you, but I couldn't see how. At two in the morning I thought I saw the way. Drunken men get strange ideas into their heads. You were the apple of the mother's eyes; I was only her son. No use denying it. She worshiped you; tolerated me. I came back to the house, packed up what I absolutely needed, and took the first train west. It all depended upon what you'd do. You let me go, Arty, old boy. I suppose you were pretty well knocked up, when you learned what I had done. And then you let things drift. It was only natural. I had opened the way for you. Mother, learning that I was a thief, restored the defalcation to save the family honor, which was your future. We were always more or less hard-pressed for funds. I did not gamble, but I wasted a lot. The mother gave us an allowance of five thousand each. To this I managed to add another five and you another four. You were always borrowing from me. I never questioned what you did with it. I would to God I had! It would have saved us a lot of trouble."

The hand in his relaxed and slipped from the clasp.

"Some of these things will sound bitter, but the

heart behind them isn't. So I did what I thought to be a great and glorious thing. I was sober when I reached Chicago. I saw my deed from another angle. Think of it; we could have given our joint note to mother's bank for the amount. Old Henderson would have discounted it in a second. It was too late. I went on. The few hundreds I had gave out. I've been up against it pretty hard. There were times when I envied the pariah-dog. But fortune came around one day, knocked, and I let her in. I returned to make a restitution, only to learn that it had been made by you, long ago. A trick of young Elmore's. I shouldn't have come back if I could have sent the money."

Arthur raised his head and sat up. " Ah, why did you not write? Why did you not let me know where you were? God is my witness, if there is a corner of this world unsearched for you. For two years I had a man hunting. He gave up. I believed you dead."

" Dead? Well, I was in a sense."

" You have suffered, but not as I have. Always you had before you your great, splendid, foolish sacrifice. I had nothing to buoy me up; there was only the drag of the recollection of an evil deed, and a moment of pitiful weakness. The temptation was too great, Paul."

" How did it happen? "

" How does anything like that happen? Curiosity drew me first, for at college I never played but a few games of bridge. Curiosity, desire, then the full blaze of the passion. You will never know what that is, Paul. It is stronger than love, or faith, or honor. God knows I never thought myself weak; at school I was the least impetuous of the two. Everything went, and they cheated me from the start. Roulette and faro. Then I put my hand in the safe. To this day I can not tell why. I owed nothing to those despicable thieves, Craig least of all."

" Craig. I met him over there. Pummeled him."

" I didn't act like a man. Some day a comfortable fortune would fall to the lot of each of us. But I took eight thousand, lost it, and came whining to you. You don't belong to this petty age, Paul. You ought to have been a fellow of the Round Table." Arthur smiled wanly. " To throw

your life away like that, for a brother who wasn't
fit to lace your shoes! If you had written you
would have learned that everything was smoothed
over. The Andes people dropped the matter entirely. You loved the mother far better than I."

" And she must never know," quietly.

" Do you mean that?"

" I always mean everything I say, Arty. Can't
you see the uselessness of telling her now? She
has gone all these years with the belief that I am
a thief. A thief, Arty, I, who never stole anything
save a farmer's apples. They would have called
you a defaulter; that's because you had access to the
safe, whereas I had none." Arthur winced. " I
don't propose to disillusion the mother. I am strong
enough to go away without seeing her; and God
knows how my heart yearns, and my ears and eyes
and arms."

Warrington reached mechanically for the portrait in the silver frame, but Arthur stayed his
hand.

" No, Paul; that is mine."

Warrington dropped his hand, puzzled. " I was
not going to destroy it," ironically.

"No; but in a sense you have destroyed me. Compensation. What trifling thought most of us give that word! The law of compensation. For ten years Elsa has been the flower o' the corn for me. She almost loved me. And one day she sees you; and in that one day all that I had gained was lost, and all that you had lost was gained. The law of compensation. Sometimes we escape retribution, but never the law of compensation. Some months ago she wrote me a letter. She was always direct. It was a just letter."

A pause. Arthur gazed steadily at the portrait, while Warrington twisted his yellow beard.

"The ways of mothers are mysterious," said the latter, finally. He wondered if Arthur would confess to the blacker deed, or have it forced from him. He would wait and see. "The father and the mother weren't happy. Money. There's the wedge. It's in every life somewhere. A marriage of convenience is an unwise thing. When we were born the mother turned to us. Up to the time we were six or seven there was no distinction in her love for us. But on the day the father set his choice upon me, she set hers upon you. You'll never know how I suffered as a boy, when I saw the distance growing wider and wider with the years. Perhaps the father understood, for he was always kind and gentle to me. I expect to return to China shortly. The Andes has taken me back. Sounds like a fairy-tale; eh? I shall never return here. But did you know who Elsa Chetwood was?"

" Not until that letter came."

Neither of them heard the faint gasp which came from behind the portières dividing the study and the living-room. The gasp had followed the invisible knife-thrusts of these confidences. The woman behind those portières swayed and caught blindly at the jamb. With cruel vividness she saw in this terrible moment all that to which she had never given more than a passing thought. No reproaches; only a simple declaration of what had burned in this boy's heart. And she had almost forgotten this son. A species of paralysis laid hold of her, leaving her for the time incapable of movement.

She heard the deep voice of this other son say: " Lots of kinks in life. There is only one law that I shall lay down for you, Arty. You must give up all idea of marrying Elsa Chetwood."

"It will be easy to obey that. Are you playing with me, Paul?"

"Playing?" echoed Warrington.

"Yes. Do you mean to sit there and tell me that you don't know why I shall never marry her?"

"Arty, I don't understand what you're talking about."

Arthur read the truth in his brother's eyes. He smiled weakly, the anger gone. "Same old blind duffer you always were. I wrote an answer to her letter. In that letter I told her . . . the truth."

"You did that?"

"I am your brother, Paul. I couldn't be a cad as well as a thief. Yes, I told her. I told her more, what you never knew. I let Craig believe that I was you, Paul. I wore your clothes, your scarf-pins, your hats. In that I was a black villain. God! What a hell I lived in. . . . Ah, mother!" Arthur dropped his head upon his arms again.

"Paul, my son!"

It was Warrington's chair that toppled over. Framed in the portières stood his mother, white-haired, pale but as beautiful as of old.

"I am sorry. I had hoped to get away without your knowing."

"Why?"

"Oh, because there wasn't any use of my coming at all. I'd passed out of your life, and I should have stayed out. Don't worry. I've got everything mapped out. There's a train at midnight."

Arthur stood up. "Mother, I am the guilty man. I was the thief. All these years I've let you believe that Paul had taken the money. . . ."

"Yes, yes!" she interrupted, never taking her eyes off this other son. "I heard everything behind these curtains. You were going away, Paul, without seeing me?"

"What was the use of stirring up old matters? Of bringing confusion into this house?" He did not look at her. He could not tell her that he now knew what had drawn him hither, that all along he had deceived himself.

"Paul, my son, I have been a wicked woman."

"Why, mother, you mustn't talk like that!"

"Wicked! My son, my silent, kindly, chivalric boy, will you forgive your mother? Your unnatural mother?"

He caught her before her knees touched the floor; and, ah! how hungrily her arms wound about him.

"What's the use of lying?" he cried brokenly. " My mother! I wanted to hear your voice and feel your arms. You don't know how I have always loved you. It was a long time, a very long time. Perhaps I was to be blamed. I was proud, and kept away from you. Don't cry. There, there! I can go away now, happy." Over his mother's shoulders, now moving with silent stabbing sobs, he held out his hand to his brother. Presently, above the two bowed heads, Warrington's own rose, transfigured with happiness.

The hall-door opened and closed, but none of them regarded it.

By and by the mother stood away, but within arm's length. " How big and strong you have grown, Paul."

" In heart, too, mother," added Arthur. " Old Galahad!"

" You must never leave us again, Paul. Promise."

" May I always come back?"

HE THAT WAS DEAD

"Always!" And she took his hand and pressed it tightly against her cheek. "Always! Ah, your poor blind mother!"

"Always to come back! . . . I am going to China in a little while, to take up the work I have always loved, the building of bridges."

"And I am going, too!" It was Elsa, at her journey's end.

Jealous love is keen of eye. There was death in Arthur's heart, but he smiled at her. After all, what was more logical than that she should appear at this moment? Why sip the cup when it might be drained at once, over with and done with?

"Elsa!" said the mother, holding Warrington's hand in closer grasp.

"Yes, mother. Ah, why did you not tell me all?"

Arthur walked to the long window that opened out upon the garden. There, for a moment, he paused, then passed from the room.

"Go to him, mother," said Elsa, wisely and with pity.

The mother hesitated, pulled by the old and the new love, by the fear that the new-found could be hers but a little while. Slowly she let Paul's hand fall, and slower still she followed Arthur's footsteps.

"I wasn't quite brave enough," he said, when she found him. "They love. And love me well, mother, for I am the broken man."

She pressed his head against her heart. "My boy!" But her glance was leveled at the amber-tinted window through which she had come.

To Warrington, Elsa was a little thinner, and of color there was none; but her eyes shone with all the splendor of the Oriental stars at which he had so often gazed with mute inquiry.

"Galahad!" she said, and smiled. "Well, what have you to say?"

"I? In God's name, what can I say but that I love you?"

"Well, say it, and stop the ache in my heart! Say it, and make me forget the weary eighteen thousand miles I have journeyed to find you! Say it, and hold me close for I am tired! . . . Listen!" she whispered, lifting her head from his shoulder.

From out the stillness of the summer night came a jarring note, the eternal protest of Rajah.

THE END.